Around the World in Stilettos

by Natalie-Jane Revell

Around the world IN Stilettos

HandE Publishers Ltd

Published by HandE Publishers Ltd
Epping Film Studios, Brickfield Business Centre,
Thornwood High Road, Epping, Essex, CM16 6TH
www.handepublishers.co.uk

First published in the United Kingdom 2010
First Edition

ISBN 978-1-906873-40-0
A CIP catalogue record for this book is available from
The British Library

Copyright © Text Natalie-Jane Revell 2010
Cover design by Ruth Mahoney
Typeset by Ruth Mahoney
Edited by Kayleigh Hart and Sarah Cheeseman

Printed and bound in England
by CPI Bookmarque, Croydon, Surrey

To Mum and Dad
and Lyndhurst times

Other titles to come in the 'Foot Loose' series:

Around the World in Flip-Flops
Around the World in Ski's

Acknowledgments

I have so many people to thank, who have supported and guided me through writing and publishing my first novel.

Firstly, I'd like to thank Kayleigh, because without her none of you would even be able to read the book, as you would have passed out from lack of breath after the first page due to my lack of full stops.

Of course, Justine, the whole publishing team and the graphics team at HandE, who believed in me and my story, I just hope they had as much fun helping to get it to print as I had writing it.

My family, for giving me so much inspiration and guidance, especially my little brother Ben, who is always trying to make me a better person, and my nan.

Of course the bank of mum and dad also helped. I wouldn't really have got anywhere without them - well actually, that's a given, seeing as I wouldn't even be here without them! And I definitely wouldn't be the person I am today if it wasn't for them.

Then to my friends, who, as well as sharing all my ups and downs, have encouraged me to reach my goals, and so this is as much their victory as it is mine. Elize, for finding the only copy of the first draft on my computer when I thought I had lost it, and teaching me the importance of backing up my work. Rhys and Andrew, for giving me countless tales to write about as we travelled through Europe together, and yes Rhys, you can have a mention for helping me come up with the title. Mark, of course, for just being you, and for making sure I didn't give up. You believed in me constantly, as did all at Lyndhurst, and I am eternally grateful.

Emma and Justin, you always believed in me and kept encouraging me to keep going, and without your wedding to draw inspiration from, the book wouldn't be the same. The rest of you I won't name, but you know who you are and you have all helped me in your own way.

To every other beautiful person who has helped me - there are hundreds of you out there, from school to uni to work - you have all had a vital role to play in making this possible.

I love you all, and thank you.

Acknowledgments

Chapter One
Dating Agencies and Drinks

I feel slightly apprehensive as I walk down the stairs towards the doors of the almost hidden room. Pushing through them, I sit on the stool and begin to talk. Not exactly the way I thought dating agencies worked, but what do I know?

"A life lived by other people. A life defined by other people's decisions and rules. That was never really my idea of much of a life at all, if I'm totally honest! Which is also the precise reason for my determination never to end up in a nine-to-five office job somewhere, and well, so far I think I've definitely achieved that! Oh sorry, is that okay?" I look over at the woman behind the camera, flushing slightly, and smiling awkwardly. Oh shit, why did I let Emily talk me into doing this! My brain is overloading with embarrassment at the whole experience. I mean a dating agency, I'm twenty-three for God's sake! I really should learn to say no to her ideas – they're always getting me into trouble!

"That's fine, Miss Farrier," the trim middle-aged woman says, forcing a smile which doesn't quite mask her impatience.

I look around the small, dimly lit room, trying to regain my composure. Why am I doing this? I know I've not exactly had the best luck with romance, well okay, so it's been pretty dismal really – my last boyfriend turned out to be married – and let's just say I have a knack for falling for the wrong blokes. But still, I'm only twenty-three – it will happen for me soon, it's not like I'm quite past it yet. I hope.

"Miss Farrier." The woman is growing more impatient as she wakes me from my reverie.

"Sorry, I was having a bit of an epiphany," I try to joke, unsuccessfully, with her, as she just glares sternly at me.

"Miss Farrier, you should probably tell them your name now, I do have five more women to see this morning!" she says in an agitated tone.

"Really?" I reply, quite shocked that there are that many women around London who have as much bad luck with men as I do. Realising that I hadn't exactly hidden this shock I add, too late, "I… I thought you would have had more! I mean, it's impossible to find a man these days, isn't it?" As I expected, she isn't convinced. Oh, this experience really is getting worse by the minute, and if I'm not mistaken I'm pretty sure that smell is getting stronger.

Once again, I glance around the musty room. Thinking about it, this doesn't really seem like the sort of dating agency they have in the movies, more like a shady video shop backroom. I read somewhere the other day that all the celebrities are using exclusive dating agencies at the moment, and I have to admit that I did kind of picture myself in one of those, not a basement. This thought makes me shudder ever so slightly and I become suddenly aware of the woman glaring at me again. Okay, better get this over and done with before she hits me or something.

"Erm… so my name's Sophie Farrier, I'm twenty-three and live just outside of London. I'm a travel writer so spend a lot of time away from home, so I guess I'm looking for a guy who is flexible and likes to travel." I pause and try to suppress my giggles as I realise how stupid I look. I swear I'm just copying dialogue straight out of an episode of some comedy sketch show now! Honestly, this whole thing is bound to come back and bite me on the arse one day; it will be on one of those 'before they were famous' programmes, and they'll dig out this video and show it on national television. Oh crap, I've really got to work on stopping this daydreaming in public, no wonder people look at me like I'm crazy. They probably think I've been smoking pot all morning or something.

"So, is that alright?" I ask pleadingly.

"Yes, Miss Farrier, that's fine," she sighs, not even bothering to hide her relief.

Great! I can finally leave, which is good seeing as that smell is starting to make me feel a bit woozy now – I wonder what it is? I pick up my bag and walk out of the room in a manner that is as dignified as I can possibly manage after such a humiliating experience (such as speaking a load of rubbish into a video camera to be relayed to the sort of men I'm not at all sure I even want to meet!). When I reach the street I breathe in the fresh air – well, as fresh as London air gets anyway. I disappear into the

3

busy underground station with this thought still in my mind, and wearily make my way home.

* * *

Three hours later, I am still not quite over the embarrassment as I sit on the old couch in the small flat Emily and I share, nibbling on a large chocolate bar, and waiting for Emily to come home so I could kill her. I look up when I hear the creak of her opening the door, and turn down the TV. Emily comes strolling in, humming the theme tune to 'The O.C.' and dumps her bag in the small hallway, which is already crowded with shoes and coats as well as being cluttered with a small nest of tables (a gift from my parents).

"I can't believe how busy it's been today," she says, as she walks into the combined living and dining room and drops her dishevelled form down in the armchair.

"How can it be busy? You look at bones that have been dug up and give them to someone to put down in the museum for a living!" I ask in bewilderment.

"Sophie, you don't realise how much goes into archaeology and authenticating items everyday, it's very hard work, especially if they've come from a big dig or an unreliable source." She sounded quite indignant and I sensed a quick change of subject might be in order, so time, I think, to mention my disastrous day.

"So anyway," I interject, "I've had a bloody awful day too, you know," looking pointedly at her. I continue, "It was something to do with that stupid dating agency thing you convinced me to do!"

"Oh shit! Sorry, Sophie, I completely forgot about that, how did it go?" she says, looking slightly guilty while trying to hide her giggles behind the back of her hand as I explain the whole disastrous event in detail – going quite red at recalling it all again. "Okay, okay. I'm sorry," she says at last. "How about I make you dinner to make up for it?"

"You, make me dinner!" I laugh incredulously.

"Oh alright, I'll order Indian – we haven't had one for ages," she laughs back, "but I think I may need a shower first." She then gets up and heads towards the bathroom.

"Aw, no order it now or it won't be delivered until midnight by the time you've finished in the shower," I say pleadingly.

"Oh okay then," she sighs walking to the table and routing through the drawer to find the menu. "What do you want then?" she asks sitting back down with the phone in one hand and the menu in the other.

"Hmm," I pause thinking hard about this important decision, "I think the same old, same old, chicken Korma," I laugh as she gives me a withering look the phone already to her ear, "What?" I say giggling, so maybe I do order the same thing every time but you never know do you I might suddenly change my mind.

"Right done," she says throwing the phone down on the chair as she stands up again and starts heading towards the door.

"Yeah well, don't think you're getting away with it that easily – it was a bloody awful day, Em, so you can do the washing up for a week to make up for it!"

Ignoring me completely, she carries on walking.

"Maybe next time I'll just set you up with one of Sam's

friends!" she calls back to me, as she disappears round the door back into the corridor before I can launch a cushion in her direction.

Sam is Emily's boyfriend/fiancé (their status changes every time they talk about it!). Very good looking, rich, but actually I think he's a bit boring really. He does, however, have an impeccable taste in clothes, always looks perfect and nearly always wears a suit (as most lawyers do, I suppose). But I'm not really interested in meeting one of his hot but boring mates; personally, I'm still holding out for Orlando Bloom to come and ask me to marry him.

*   *   *

Half an hour later a ring on the doorbell awakens me from my daydreaming of Orlando Bloom meeting me at the end of the aisle on our wedding day, and I must say I was wearing the most gorgeous shoes ever, I have to find out if a pair like that exist in real life, and I get up to answer the door.

I walk slowly towards the front door and can hear the muffled sounds of Emily singing in the shower. I open the door to Sam and smile briefly as he greets me, before turning back towards the living room, Sam following at his usual relaxed pace. As he sits down I marvel once more at his amazing dress sense; this evening he is wearing a well-fitting pair of Levis and a tight pale-yellow shirt, Armani I think. Flushing slightly, I realise I've been staring a little too hard and too long at him and look away quickly. Mental note to self: STOP doing that!

"So, Sophie, how's your day been?" he asks politely.

"Oh fine thanks, how about you? Any big important cases going on at the moment?" I reply, equally as polite.

"Well there is one case, it's rather interesting actually," he pauses and then launches into a story full of legal jargon, which isn't interesting at all. In fact, I'm lost already and just smile and nod occasionally as I daydream once more about Orlando Bloom. The doorbell rings again and this time I jump up a little more eagerly to answer it.

"That'll be the food," I say to Sam. "Yes, escape!" I mutter to myself as I approach the door. "Em! Have you got any cash?" I call out, as I take the bag of food from the delivery man.

"In my bag," she yells from behind her bedroom door. Wow! That's the quickest shower she has ever had, I think to myself as I rifle around for her purse. Finding it, I eventually pay the poor man after trying to offer him a combination of euros and pesos, as well as some ancient-looking Roman-type coin first. Shutting the door I head towards the kitchen, just as Emily walks into the living room looking fresh-faced and awake again.

"Hello, darling," she says, greeting Sam with a kiss as she heads for her food. Clearing a space on the surface of our kitchen counter I uncover the food, as Emily is busy searching for a couple of clean dishes amongst the mess.

Finally, we sit down in front of an old episode of 'Friends' and tuck in. As we eat, I mention that I'll get round to cleaning the kitchen tomorrow after I've dropped Emily off at the station.

"Speaking of work, Soph, have you booked those tickets yet?" asks Emily curiously.

"Shit, no, I'll do that after dinner," I say reassuringly.

"How is the magazine, Sophie?" Sam asks from the sofa, not

quite taking his eyes off the television.

"Oh it's fantastic thanks, I love the travelling."

It's true actually, my job's amazing. I write for a travel magazine, travelling to all kinds of interesting places and being paid not only to travel there but to write about the experience, too. Oh yes, and did I mention that the person I travel the world with, and who writes the adjoining article to mine, just happens to be a tall, dark and handsome man of twenty-five?

Only problem being he has a perfectly beautiful girlfriend already – no harm in looking though, is there? As my friend once said 'you don't get fat from looking at the chocolate'. Mind you although I stuck to that philosophy for a long time, I did make the mistake of changing the rules once. I was in a supermarket one day and thought to myself, as you do, maybe there's no rule against smelling 'the chocolate' either, and well basically to cut a long story short, I got caught sniffing this gorgeous bloke who was standing in front of me in the queue. I won't go in to details but let's just say I was lucky there were no restraining orders involved and I don't go back there anymore!

After spending a couple of minutes picturing myself kissing Dan on a white sandy beach, I open a bottle of wine and retire with it to my room and sit at my computer. I begin typing an email to Dan; he's so hot… seriously, he has the nicest arse in existence.

We're off to Rome for three days next week and I was supposed to be booking the tickets, but to be honest I've lost… no, that's not right… I've temporarily misplaced my copy of the details. Actually, they might be under that pile of stuff on the floor by my desk; oh, I can't be bothered to look now, Dan can book the tickets while I'm cleaning tomorrow. With that thought in mind, I click the send button and head back towards the living room. Emily and Sam have gone out, so I pour myself another glass of wine, settle down and flick through the channels until 'America's Next Top Model' comes on.

Chapter Two
Cocktails at dawn

I wake up the next morning with my head swimming just a little; maybe it was a bad idea to finish off that bottle of wine last night. I sink my head back down into the warm pillow and turn over to go back to sleep, but looking at the clock I see it's half seven and I can hear Emily in the shower. So, reluctantly, I drag myself out of bed and pull on a pair of jogging bottoms and a tank top, and walk into the kitchen to pour myself a cup of coffee.

After dropping Emily off, I scrape my hair into a ponytail and look around the flat wearily. Right, it's Friday, my last day off for the next month and it's a big night out tonight, so I'll spend the morning cleaning and the afternoon pampering. Really it should be Emily doing this after yesterday, but I think I've made her suffer enough over the years and she has cleaned the last three times, which I guess means there's no avoiding the fact that it's my turn.

So after three hours of hard scrubbing, dusting and hoovering, I finally slump down onto the sofa with a bowl of noodles and a cheese sandwich to watch a re-run of an old episode of 'Casualty' on UKTV Gold. After my lunch, and my rest, I get changed into a pair of jeans and a flowing top (because it's always best to hide our lumps and bumps if we have them, at least that's what my mum always told me and I'm inclined to agree) and head out.

Finding a parking space in town was easier than I thought, and as I pay for my ticket I realise how much I love my hometown, even if it does seem like a dump to everyone else. But in all my travels I've never found anywhere that gives me that same warm glow as the place I was brought up in. As I reminisce about my childhood, I walk towards the salon to get my acrylic nails filled in and airbrushed with a new pattern.

* * *

Later that afternoon in my bedroom, I admire the new outfit I accidentally bought on the way back to the car, before hopping into the shower. Sitting in front of the mirror I comb through my long blonde hair, which really does need a cut, and try to decide how to wear it tonight. "Down I think, and straight," I say aloud to myself.

"Soph, can I borrow those black stilettos?" comes Emily's voice, as she bustles into my room half-dressed and flings my wardrobe doors open, at which point a pile of clothes falls on her knocking her flying onto my bed. "Bloody hell, Soph, where did all these come from?" she splutters, uncovering herself.

"Erm… they're just bits and bobs from home and shops and stuff," I stutter back sheepishly.

"Well, I'm borrowing this top for starters," she giggles, admiring a blue lace-up evening top. I just roll my eyes knowing it'll never fit her anyway – too big by about three sizes – and turn back to the mirror.

* * *

Two and a half hours later we're finally ready, Emily looking stunning in a pair of very tight dark-blue jeans (size eight – small, I know!) and a low-cut red sequined top. Honestly, when you see her looking like that, it's hard to imagine her spending her days in dusty combat trousers messing around with bones. Her short blonde hair straight and looking perfect, minimal make-up complementing her blue eyes, oh, and to top it off she's wearing my beautiful, stunning, amazing black satin stilettos (eighty-five pounds from Oasis, what a bargain!).

I, on the other hand, am wearing a pair of light-blue jeans (size fourteen) and my brand new low-cut halter-neck backless black top. My hair curly (changed my mind again) and my usual reasonably heavy but sexy black eye make-up, which brings out the blue in my eyes (well, I think so anyway). To complete the outfit, a new pair of black wedge shoes I bought the other day on my way home from work.

Okay, so I have a bit of a shoe fetish, but that's perfectly normal. I mean, I read somewhere the other day that the average woman spends eight thousand pounds on shoes in her lifetime.

Besides, when you don't have a size eight figure, shoes are the perfect substitute for all the lovely clothes you can't buy. Okay, okay, so I may have a tiny clothes fetish too, and well, if I'm completely honest, I just like buying things that I think make me look good.

"You coming, Soph?" calls Emily from the hallway. "The taxi's waiting," she says again, slightly more impatiently.

"Okay, I'm just coming," I yell back, and taking a final glance at myself in my wardrobe mirror I hurry out, closing the door behind me.

* * *

Sitting in the bar, I sip on what must be my fifth double vodka and orange, and can feel my head starting to spin just a little as I try and focus on the conversation going on around me. Emily is sitting with Sam and there are two of his friends here too – one of them is quite hot actually. Oh shit, he just asked me something, concentrate, Sophie, focus.

"Sorry, I didn't quite catch that," I say rather thickly, trying to focus on his face. What was his name again? Something beginning with a D I think… Dave, Danny? No Dean, that's it, Dean!

"I was just asking what you did for a living," he replied patiently, staring a little too intently at my breasts as he spoke. Men, honestly, will they never learn to look a woman in the eyes?

"Oh, I'm a travel writer actually," I say proudly. I love talking about my job to anyone who will listen; I feel like it's only a couple of notches down from being famous. It's fair to say that I'm the only one that thinks this, but they're still interested to hear about it (honestly!). Dean, however, only seems interested in staring at my boobs and touching up my leg under the table.

"Right, well, I'm just going to nip to the loo quickly," I say a little too loudly, as half the bar turn to look at me. I make a quick and ungraceful exit, stumbling over a bag on the way. By the time I get to the loo my face is flushed the deep crimson of embarrassment mixed with drunkenness. Oh well, I think to myself, it's not like I'll remember much of this that clearly in the morning. I pull out my bronzer and apply some to disguise my now flaming red cheeks. Slowly, I walk back towards the table at the back of the bar, but Emily grabs me and drags me towards the bar first.

"My round, I think," she grins, as she hails the barman over and orders a pitcher of some cocktail for the two of us and three pints of Fosters for the boys. She drops a load of coins on the floor and chuckles as she attempts to pick them up, showing that she's just as pissed as me. Together, we walk back to the table, sloshing beer, and a blue liquid we were told was a cocktail, all over the place on the way. Sitting down again, I pour out a drink and immediately feel what's-his-name's hand on my thigh! The night continued like this, but early on I had decided not to take this further, partly because I was too drunk to even remember his name, but mostly because he was far too uncomplicated for me to get involved with. So the poor bloke was fighting a losing battle on that front. But we all laughed and joked and had a generally good night until the bar finally closed at midnight and the five of us stumbled out. Saying our farewells, we split up.

Emily, Sam and I head for our cab home and the other two disappear in the opposite direction. Reaching home, I spend at least five giggling minutes trying to fit the key into the lock before entering the dark flat and collapsing on the sofa in a drunken stupor.

* * *

At around seven o'clock in the morning I open my eyes and look around blurrily, still on the sofa, the early spring sun shining through the open curtains. Oh crap! I should really stop drinking, my head is banging. I stumble to my room, grab a towel and head to the shower. An hour later, I feel refreshed and the smoke and sticky alcohol of last night has been washed from my hair and skin. Putting my clothes in the wooden washing basket, which sits in the corner of our bathroom, I wrap my large bath towel around me, fix my hair with a smaller towel into a turban-like arrangement and head back to my room. Brushing my hair I tie it up loosely, figuring that turning on my hairdryer would wake up Emily and Sam, and after moisturising, slip into a comfy pair of old jeans and loose top – my usual Saturday attire – and switch on my computer. Turning around I begin to clean my room while I wait for it to load. Pushing clothes back into my wardrobe I find my powder-pink sequined tank-top.

"Brilliant," I say aloud, "I've been looking for this for ages!" Folding it up, I put it in the half-full open suitcase sitting in the corner by my window. Right, so that's all my packing nearly done then, except the shoes Emily wore last night. The only downside of my job is that it's not always that glamorous. In fact, the truth is, I always pack all my beautiful clothes and spend most of the time traipsing around tourist sites in walking boots and shorts, sweating tons and jotting down everything I can understand in my notebook, before going back to the hotel, or villa. I then spend the night writing up the notes, eating something and then collapsing into bed ready to get up at dawn and start all over again. This time, however, it will be different and I can't wait. The magazine had decided to do a feature piece on how the 'other half' lived, and this meant that for three days I was to be wined, dined and escorted around in luxury.

You see, Dan and I have made our names in the travel writing world by becoming freelance writers on our magazine, and last year our editor had decided to put in a piece that was to investigate the opposing views of men and women on a sightseeing holiday in China. We were the two chosen to write the pieces. It was hugely successful and, as they say, the rest is history! Now, everywhere we go, we write our separate articles on how we feel as a man or woman about wherever we are and they are published opposite each other. A couple of months ago we were even invited to go on 'GMTV' to talk about our travels, but that won't actually take place for another few months, although I'll admit that the outfit I bought for it has been hanging in my wardrobe since the day I got the call! It's all a bit of a whirlwind really. No one expected any of it to be successful, not to this extent anyway, but there you have it! The public love to read where a good place for a couple to go is, I suppose, and also what there is to do there.

But anyway, back to the point… what was the point? I don't really think there was one come to think of it, but I carry on tidying until my room resembles something slightly like a clean bedroom – organised chaos, I like to call it. I then proceed to do some research on the net for my forthcoming trip; this consists of looking up all the expensive hotels and resorts in Rome and cooing over all the facilities and luxuries, before gasping over the prices and jotting it all down messily in my new notebook. I buy a new notebook for every trip I make and on top of my wardrobe I have a box full of all my used ones – I use them sometimes as references – usually just cheap little ones to jot stuff down in as I traipse from place to place. But to mark the fact that this time I was going in style, I had spent a little extra (well, quite a lot extra really) on a leather-bound A5 notebook, and yes, okay, it cost me just over ten pounds… okay, it cost nineteen ninety-nine, but it was worth it and I already feel a little more sophisticated just writing the details in it.

* * *

After a couple of hours I can hear Emily and Sam moving around and venture out to find some breakfast and make a cup of coffee for the pair of them. Now the thing about Emily is that she functions primarily on coffee, but it has to be good coffee, so after months of practising I have finally perfected my coffee-making skills. Using the big metal robot-type machine, which apparently needs to be as big as half our kitchen and makes the sound of a road being ripped up, I can succeed in making a small cup of cappuccino. But anyway, I had tackled and defeated the robot-type machine and could hear Sam and Emily emerging, as I set the mugs on the tray and carried them through to the living room.

"Ah cheers, Soph, you're a star," they both mumble, laughing at their hung-over state. I retreat to find my bowl of oat granola before joining them to watch some 'Family Guy' (a tradition we have following a drunken Friday night!). We sit dozing for a while and laughing at the TV until about two o'clock, when Sam decided that it was about time he went home and did some paperwork. I marvel at that man, really I do, talk about dedicated – he's always working, probably a swot at school as well, but I suppose it paid off. I mean, he's already a junior partner at his firm.

"Hey, Em, what are we doing tonight?" I sigh, moving my head to look at her with the minimum amount of effort.

"Oh, I was thinking a girly night in. I bought some face packs the other day and we have a few chick flicks around to watch." She didn't even look over at me but could sense my small nod, and we then continued to slob out for the remainder of the afternoon.

* * *

The night draws in slowly as we sit around chatting and eating; it is shaping up to be a typical Saturday evening until the phone rings. Reaching for it, Emily picks it up before calling to me.

"Sophie, it's Dan, for you."

Running over to the phone, I take it from her, bemused as to why he is phoning me at half nine on a Saturday night.

"Hello Dan, what's up?"

Dan's voice was rushed and he sounded angry...

"Sophie, didn't you get my email? I've just had the Editor on the phone about the tickets!"

Oh SHIT! Bollocks, I'm in so much trouble, crap, crap, crap. Clearing my throat a little I simply reply:

"What exactly is the problem? Can't we book the tickets now? I mean, it's just a simple mistake!" I look pleadingly at the receiver as if he can see my face down it.

Emily meanwhile has turned the volume down and is listening intently to my dilemma.

"No, we can't just book them now because the hotel's booked for Monday night and there are no available first-class flights, and in case you'd forgotten, we have to travel first class to write the article!" He was getting angrier with me and my face was burning as I felt hot tears prickling in the back of my eyes.

My mind racing, I breathe heavily, trying to calm my shaking voice, until suddenly a spark ignites and a plan forms (I really do love the way my brain works under pressure, don't know what I'd do without it!).

"It's okay, come over to mine now and I think I can sort it out, I have a plan," I say, my voice still shaking.

"I hate your plans, but okay, this better work," he sounds slightly calmer, more like the Dan I was used to.

"Cool, see you in about twenty minutes then," I say hurriedly.

"Okay. Oh, and Soph, I'm sorry for yelling but you really are a twat sometimes," he says before cutting off.

I put down the phone sighing, then look over at Emily laughing at me and fling a pillow at her before running off to do my make-up.

Okay, so I can do this. Simple. Why didn't I think of it before? It's perfect! Finishing my mascara and changing my top I enter the living room to get the verdict. Twirling, I wait for comments.

"Very hot but casual, as if you've been caught off guard but still look amazing," Emily giggles, and I smile as I sink into the couch next to her and nick a chocolate. "I don't know why you bother, you know," she says to me, as the theme tune for 'The Ghost Whisperer' starts playing in the background.

"Why? Because he has a beautiful girlfriend who I can't possibly compete with?" I say, turning towards her.

"No, because you spend your working days travelling all over with him and looking very sweaty with no make-up on." She ducks as I attempt to hit her with another cushion.

"Ah, but my dear, this time I can set my plan in motion. You see, we are already good friends and I have gained his trust, which means information, like the fact that there are troubles in paradise. Oh, and to finish it off, on this trip we are to look gorgeous all the time and then he'll just have to fall in love with me!"

We both laugh and begin quoting stupid lines from chick flicks, when the doorbell rings. Still giggling, I make my way to the door and open it, letting a bedraggled Dan in. I hadn't even realised it was raining, but he stood in front of me soaking wet.

"Ah babe, you're soaked," I say sympathetically.

"No shit," he replied irritably. I blush slightly as I take his jacket and hang it on the back of the door.

"Sorry," I say quietly, "come in, I'll get you a drink." I walk towards the living room and he follows me after removing his shoes, and sits tentatively on the edge of the armchair as I continue through to the kitchen to make him a cup of tea.

"You alright, sweetheart?" Emily asks him kindly, as she offers him a chocolate.

"Yeah, fine thanks, how's work going? Found any interesting artefacts recently?" he replied warmly. The pair of them chatted for a while – they had always got on, but then she didn't have to work with him…

Entering the living room again I hand him a mug of tea and some biscuits, and I usher him into my room with Emily winking at me over his shoulder. Laughing, I give her the finger and a smile before shutting the door behind us.

"So," he says sceptically, perching on the end of my bed, "what's the big plan?"

Taking a deep breath, I launch into my plan at top speed, hardly pausing for breath.

"Well, I was reading something the other day about this rich couple travelling by private jet that went from their private airfield to pretty much anywhere in the world they wanted to go. I looked it up and there's one that is owned by that rich old bloke who was chatting me up at the last dinner thing we were at, remember? Well, what if we phone him and ask if we could borrow his plane for a bit? Not just going first class but by private jet, just to make it completely different from the way we usually do it." Finishing, I hold my breath, waiting for his response as he thinks the plan over.

"A private jet?" he asks incredulously.

"Yeah well, it's kind of a small plane type thing I think, but definitely rich person's transport, which is what we're supposed to write about," I say, starting to doubt my own plan.

"Wait a minute, Chloe's parents have a plane. If we can borrow it and hire a pilot we can cut down the price of travel, and I think it will be perfect to pitch to Marie tomorrow!" He sounds more excited as he flips open his phone and speaks to his 'perfect' girlfriend.

A plane! Is there anything this girl didn't have? I mean, a fucking jet! Shaking my head I realise that I'm still gaping open-mouthed over this fact, and I look at him hopefully as he tries to secure the loan of their plane for tomorrow, promising all kinds of things in return. He closes the phone and looks over at me solemnly for a minute – my heart skips a beat. Oh, we are really screwed now, but then his mouth cracks into a smile as he tells me we have it. I launch a pillow at him, pretending to punch him.

"Don't do that, I nearly died then!" I gasp before straightening up. "Damn!" I exclaim suddenly.

"What? What is it?" he asks, shocked at my sudden outburst.

"I have to pack a whole extra load of stuff for the plane trip now by tomorrow morning and I need to wash half of it," I say in dismay.

He just laughs at me, hitting me playfully over the back of the head as he gets up. Seeing him to the door, I confirm details with him until finally agreeing that he was to pick me up from the flat at half nine the next morning, where we would head straight to the office (I know, it's open on a Sunday, ridiculous isn't it? But there we go, it's a twenty-four-seven job I suppose!).

We would then go to the private jet, wherever that was, and off on our latest business trip. I hope it all goes okay because, well, I've left it to him now. At least I can blame him if it doesn't go okay but I don't want him to hate me, after all if he does, my plan of getting him has hit a serious snag!

"So!" Emily turns to me inquisitively, scanning me for every detail.

"I messed up big time, Em!" I say, pulling a face at her as I sink into the armchair.

"Well, I gathered that," was the sarcastic reply.

"It's okay, I think I've sorted it out, but he was mad. He's taken over all the arrangements and I haven't got a clue what's going on. All I know is that I have to be ready for tomorrow, which means I can't sleep tonight because I'll be doing the washing I was going to do tomorrow." I breathe in before letting out a deep sigh and grabbing the remote to change the channel. Laughing, Em gets up and walks to the bathroom. Grabbing the washing out of the basket she puts it in the machine and turns it on.

"There you go," she exclaims, "that's your first step done!" Grabbing the remote off me she switches over to the pick of the week replay of Tuesday's episode of 'Shameless'.

Chapter Three
Romance in Rome

Rome today! My head is filled with giddy excitement as I think over the prospects of the next few days. Stretching out lazily, I glance over at the clock to double check that it is seven. What! No way. It can't be half eight, my alarm was set for seven, at least I think… no, I'm sure I set it. Shit, that means I only have an hour to get ready and finish packing. Throwing off my covers I jump up, then sit straight back down again – head rush, way too much energy when I've only just woken up. After standing up more slowly, I trot as quickly as I can across the hallway in my underwear and open the bathroom door, where I am confronted with Sam's toothpaste-filled mouth. I scream as I attempt to cover myself up unsuccessfully and I can feel my face flush as we stand staring at each other in silence. As I run back to my room I can't quite work out whether it's a good thing or not that he looks like he may be more embarrassed than me!

I do love that suit on him though; blue really does bring out the colour in his eyes. Still, it would never have worked between us. I mean, aside from the fact that he's Emily's fiancé and the boring thing, but, well, there's the whole arguing thing. I mean, lawyers argue and the good ones are very good at arguing, which means as I have never lost an argument, I would simply have crushed his self-esteem. It's absolutely nothing to do with the fact that he is out of my league and has a better dress sense than I do! I should have been a lawyer really but I couldn't have dealt with all those boring suits. That and the punctuality thing – never my strongest point. Now where was I? Oh yes, shower. Crap, it's eight forty-five already, Dan is going to kill me, I'll never be ready on time.

* * *

Okay, so showered, hair sort of dried, stuff packed, my make-up is sort of done, I have my little see-through plastic bag with very little tubes of make-up (airline regulation size of course) and that's it, I'm done. Wow, and time to spare for a cup of tea. I sit in the kitchen sipping at my tea and nibbling on a strawberry poptart, and flip through my notebook. Okay, so the first night we have to stay in a hostel again because the hotel was fully booked until the day we were originally supposed to arrive. Just as I was about to get out another poptart my phone started to ring, telling me Dan was waiting outside for me, so I grab my suitcase and handbag, and drag them and myself down the stairs.

The office was quiet and seemed unusually clinical on the crisp Sunday morning as I sat waiting for our editor, Marie, to call us in. Dan sat next to me. He looked tired and anxious but a little happier than last night. God, I feel so guilty, but I can't help noticing that he looks so sexy in that T-shirt. Crap, I'm staring again, stop it, Sophie!

"Sophie, Dan, come in," her voice was shrill and a shiver runs down my spine as I stand up. I hope this goes well. Shaking slightly, my palms getting clammier by the second, I walk with my head down, trying to hide slightly behind Dan as he strolls confidently into the office. My breathing getting shallower, I look around the spacious office, avoiding eye contact with the tall skinny woman standing behind the desk, her hair scraped back into a tight ponytail and her face heavily made-up to try and disguise her age. Recently, she had taken to wearing turtleneck jumpers to hide the wrinkles across her neck and chest. The red one she's wearing today is tucked into her black pencil skirt, accentuating her skinniness. Her shoes are lovely though: bright-red round-toed stilettos, Dolce and Gabbana I think! Well, well, editors must earn more than I thought. I smirk slightly at this thought before realising that not only were they both looking at me but that she had just asked me something. Crap, I wasn't listening and I can feel my face flushing bright red as I fight to try and think what she could have asked, before admitting defeat and politely asking her to repeat herself.

"You are an idiot, you know," he says, turning towards me as we sit in the car half an hour later.

"Whatever, just keep your eyes on the road!" I reply in an irritated tone, staring intently out of the window at the passing cars but actually imagining him declaring his love for me. Finding reality again, I sigh and cross my arms sulkily. He smirks slightly.

"What have I done now?" he asks, glancing at me again.

"Nothing, I'm just tired that's all," I snap, not exactly ready to spill my heart to him until the time is right; I'm thinking a sunset evening in Rome. I decide to change the subject. "So, where are we going anyway?" I say more cheerfully, looking over at him as I say it, hoping he won't persist with his question.

"Biggin Hill Airport."

Is it just me or do I detect a note of sarcasm in that comment? Oh well, I can't be bothered to argue, we're on our way to Rome. I love the travelling bit of travel writing, it's so much fun. I still can't believe I get to travel all over the world and get paid for it.

I do love airports but small ones are so boring! There aren't even any shops at this one and now I have to wait for two hours in a cold, boring and very badly decorated room. I really should talk to someone about these chairs – they are totally clashing with that awful painting on the wall. I am going to kill myself if it takes any longer. I'd rather travel on a normal plane if it means this much boredom every time you travel by private jet. Oh, at last we are told we can board the plane, so I grab at Dan's arm to hurry him up in my impatience to board a private jet for the first time, but he just grunts at me and strolls behind me slowly, still with his nose in a newspaper. God, he's acting like he's spent his whole life travelling around like this. I really do need to have words with him about how his girlfriend's habits seem to rubbing off on him. Maybe I'll get him a little tipsy first so he doesn't get really angry with me and ruin all my plans.

Bloody hell, this is almost more impressive than that cathedral we visited in Prague a few weeks ago. The carpet is actual carpet; I mean, it's nicer than the carpet in my house and it's on a plane! There are a couple of seats which look like recliners, made to make you never get out of them again, and then there is a sofa, an actual sofa. The whole thing is cream, which means I am going to have to be very careful not to spill anything; maybe I should just avoid eating or drinking anything to be on the safe side. Suddenly aware that my mouth is still wide open, I shut it and move quickly to one of the seats, sinking down into the comfort of it and sighing contentedly, glancing over at Dan who smiles that smile he gets when he is amused by something I've done, usually something embarrassing or clumsy, which is a little worrying seeing as I can't remember doing anything in the last five minutes, except stare in awe at the extravagance of this thing. I know at the end of the day it's still just a tin can with wings, but this is like the Mark's and Spencer of tin cans, it's just incredible.

* * *

Two and a half hours later, I am stepping out of the luxury penthouse version of a plane – a slight step up from my usual economy cheap airline flights to say the least – and almost fall head over heels down the stairs to the concrete below. Well, what do you expect? The champagne was free and very expensive-tasting, and I was just making the most of it. Besides, it would be rude not to drink it, wouldn't it? Clambering into the back of a cab, we head off to our slightly less luxurious room for the night. It's the journeys like this that I love the most – a chance to sit and watch a different world whiz by, like watching a fast-forwarded film or something. Staring out at people going about their daily routines, I take a deep breath and ready myself for another mini adventure, the best part of my job.

It's not just seeing new places, it's meeting new people, discovering new things. No matter how many times you visit a place like this there will always be something new to unearth. Glancing across at Dan, I am more than a little disappointed to find him sitting there texting instead of appreciating what is all around him. Oh well, I guess that's his loss really, but still, he should start looking at things the way I do, maybe then he'll realise that it's not all just about money. Things can be beautiful even if they're made from nothing, or in a really good sale.

You don't always have to pay loads of money to get something amazing, I mean, take the other day for instance, I found this gorgeous little black dress and it was only ten quid. Sainsbury's, I know, who would have believed it? But they actually do some really nice stuff in there. I was just in there getting some food shopping and happened to wander into the clothes bit, and I came out with a whole holiday's worth of clothes, it was great. Anyway, where was I? Oh yes, annoyed at Dan, bloody texting that what's-her-name girlfriend, Claire, or Chloe, or bitch face – I think it might be the last one. Giggling to myself as I think this, I notice Dan eyeing me warily and quickly stifle my humour, turning to stare once again at the scenery flying past at about four hundred miles an hour.

* * *

29

At last, we're here. Oh God, it's worse than I thought, it's not even a hostel – my worst nightmare, a bloody campsite. Okay, it's alright, I can do this. So what if the apartment, cabin, room thing we're staying in sways a little violently and smells a little stale? It will be fine. At least it's not a tent. My heart had nearly stopped when we got out of the cab and saw tents dotted around, but we got this room on stilts, which is fine. I mean, we're only here for one night; I can do one night, I think!

* * *

It doesn't matter that Dan set the air-conditioning so low last night that not only is it like walking into a freezer but I think I may have actually got frostbite in a few of my toes, because tonight we will be in a beautiful five-star hotel. That reminds me, I must write to someone about the fact that they only ever put one sheet and a smelly thin blanket in these rooms. I mean, what about the people who get cold or the people sharing rooms with bloody snowmen! But I'm not going to let any of this bother me because sitting outside the cabin, thawing in the heat of the morning, I'm reminded of just where we are. One of the most romantic cities in the world; a place so packed full of culture and history that I can't not have a fantastic time.

Walking back inside, Dan's still snoring away in his bed, so I decide to pack a few things. Even though we were only here for one night I like to feel at home and comfortable, so the room was littered with my personal effects. I pack my stuff away as quietly as possible, only slightly, maybe, trying to wake him up a little bit, and failing miserably; the bloke could sleep through a stampede, in fact he almost did once. I get out my notebook, settle down on my little bed and begin to write about the experience so far and, more importantly, my expectations for the rest of the trip. After twenty minutes of writing, I put my notebook and pen down and figure that, at eight in the morning when it's about thirty degrees outside, I should be getting dressed and sitting out there instead of freezing my arse off in a smelly little cabin. I decide a change of clothes is in order, but deciding exactly which outfit to wear is a tricky thing when travelling; it is important to always fit in with the atmosphere of the place.

So let's see, clothes for Rome. It is essential to look sophisticated and elegant – got that bit – but in my job I also have to be able to spend all day walking in and out of museums, churches and tube stations. Finally, I settle on a long brown skirt, a pair of flat sandals and a white blouse, with a shawl packed in my handbag, just in case I have to cover my arms in order to enter 'The Vatican' later on.

* * *

Half past ten. My arms are crossed and I'm staring angrily out of the small, extremely hot bus window trying to stay angry at Dan, after he made me miss the earlier bus because he woke up late and still insisted on showering for over twenty minutes. However, excitement is already rising inside me and I'm finding it hard not to beam as we draw closer to the city centre, and I can see ancient monuments approaching. I clutch at Dan's arm to show him the top of the 'Vittoriano' (or the 'Wedding Cake building' as most people refer to it) as we speed past it, nearly

31

killing several people as we do so, but he's not looking. His phone is out and he's busy texting his bloody girlfriend again. Honestly, this whole experience is completely wasted on him. The bus is now drawing to a jerky halt, and so, grabbing my notebook and camera, I usher him quickly off the bus and study the map, trying to get my bearings. Half an hour later, I've given up trying to be in charge of the map reading after leading us down a back alley and very nearly being mugged by a group of ten-year-old Italian children. Dan has his SatNav out and is muttering something as he walks in the direction of the Colosseum, with me following behind trying to take everything in without losing sight of him and becoming forever lost in the 'Eternal City'.

When we finally reach the Colosseum my breath is taken away, it is so beautiful and so huge. I do marvel sometimes at the different ways in which the two of us work. He stands there, stares at it for a couple of seconds before making a few notes and wandering off to phone Chloe. Whereas ten minutes later, I'm still gawping upwards in awe of the place. I mean, it's been there hundreds and hundreds of years, and so many people have been here and died here. How can he not feel the atmosphere? Well, his loss I suppose.

I finish taking my notes and spend a little time speaking to a couple of students I found who had come over from London to do a year's study and are doing tours of the Colosseum for extra money; best Saturday job ever! I take a couple of what I think are good photographs and wander over to where Dan is sitting chatting to an old couple, and as I draw nearer realise that he is talking Italian to them. He looks up as I reach them and stands up, smiling, turning back briefly to say something, which

I'm guessing was 'goodbye' or 'nice to meet you'. Mind you, he could easily have been saying 'thanks for the sympathy, but you try telling her she has no fashion sense', and he begins to direct me towards the underground station.

"I didn't know you spoke Italian," I question him.

"Didn't you?" he replies nonchalantly.

"Clearly not, or I wouldn't have asked, would I?" Idiot.

"I just thought you would have heard me before, it's not like we've never been to Italy, is it?"

Okay fair point, but still, just because I don't always listen to everything he says all the time, surely I would have noticed him speaking a foreign language.

"Okay, just never noticed before that's all, so where are we heading now?" I ask, changing the subject quickly before he can lecture me on never listening to him.

"Vatican City," he answers absentmindedly, as he pays for our train tickets.

By the time we get there I am almost shaking with excitement and anticipation. My parents have been to Rome several times and have always told me how beautiful 'The Vatican' is, and now I was going to get the chance to see it too.

* * *

An hour later we're still queuing patiently – good job the British are so good at queuing, because it's a big part of this job really. Still, there are some street performers playing the accordion and other instruments to keep me entertained, although this does make my purse considerably lighter. Reaching the barrier, I'm surprised that they don't ask me to cover up my arms – maybe that's only in 'St Peters' – but we do have to go through the same security procedures that they have at airports before we can enter.

It's so beautiful: a whole tiny city, within a city. Every wall is covered in the most beautiful and detailed paintings, with sculptures and statues lining the hallways. My eyes are nearly bursting out of their sockets as I snap away at every new and brightly coloured painting. My neck is starting to hurt slightly as I look up to see that every inch of the ceilings is also covered with magical scenes and beautifully depicted images. Wow, it's even more spectacular than I had thought it would be. Oh shit, oops, don't let it fall, don't let it fall! The statue I had just walked into was wobbling precariously as I try to steady it, at the same time looking around to check that no one has noticed. As I take a deep breath and attempt to walk away, I notice a group of school children snapping away at my misfortune and giggling at me, so shuffling slightly more hurriedly, I disappear into a packed side room.

Okay, so not so much looking up and slightly more concentration on where I am going then, and where the hell is Dan? Actually, come to think of it, where am I? Oh not again, he just doesn't take anything in. The last time we were in Paris he managed to get the whole way through the Louvre in about two minutes flat. It was incredible really, and he still managed to write an article that seemed to suggest he had spent hours on end wandering around its vast exhibitions. So now he's disappeared again, which means I'm lost in an impossible network of rooms and hallways, being dragged along by the crowd. This is just like him. I was going to start putting my plan into action today. It would have been perfect but, as usual, he has ruined my idea before I've had a chance to start.

* * *

An hour later I emerge, my pocket full of rolls of film from 'Vatican City', a bag in hand full of little souvenirs from this little shop they had there, including a pack of postcards depicting the paintings in the 'Sistine Chapel' – essential purchases because you're not allowed to take any photos in there. Looking around I can feel the heat of the sun on my skin as I search the street for any sign of Dan. Nowhere to be found. GREAT!

* * *

I spend the next four hours traipsing from place to place on my own and, although I'm alone, I can't help but get distracted by the beauty of each great old building I see. By six o'clock, though, I'm tired and hungry and very lost. Pulling out my phone as I hop off the third bus and still in the wrong place, I try Dan's number, but only get the busy tone before it puts me through to his voicemail. I can feel panic begin to rise in the pit of my stomach. Not to worry, it's fine, I've been in this situation tons of times and I always find my way out of them in the end. Finding a bench, I sit down for a second to rest my aching feet and figure out my next move when my phone begins to blare out Enrique's new song 'Do You Know'. Answering it quickly, Dan's voice erupts down the line.

"Where are you?"

"Where are *you*?" I answer, rather annoyed that he doesn't seem to be in the least bit worried.

"I'm at the hotel; I've been waiting for you for the last two hours."

"Well, I don't exactly know where I am. I got a bit lost and forgot what the name of the hotel was!" I squeak rather meekly.

"Great. Well, you better get back here pronto, the table for dinner is booked for half eight. Can you see a street name or anything? I'll send a car."

"Well, if you hadn't walked off and bloody left me then I wouldn't be in this trouble now, would I?" I can feel tears welling up in my eyes as I shout down the phone at him. He is just so frustrating.

"If you didn't walk so bloody slowly all the time I wouldn't lose you so easily, would I?"

"You're not even going to apologise? I'm by the Colosseum by the way."

"Okay, I'll send a car to get you."

"Fine. See you at half eight for dinner then." I hang up the phone before he can say anything else and sit there fuming.

Pushing through the door of my hotel room, I slam it behind me angrily, very nearly leaving my handbag outside as I struggle to stomp into a room I don't know my way around, tripping over a small table as I do so. Reaching the bed, frustration boils over when I can't find my suitcase, and hot tears begin to spill over onto my cheeks as I give up and sob loudly, sinking down onto the soft mattress. I can't seem to stop them as sob after sob escapes me, and before I know it my pillow is soaked, my eyes swollen and my throat sore from emotion as I yawn and drift into a restless power nap. Twenty minutes later, I awake to a knock on my door as my suitcase arrives and I realise that I should probably be getting ready. Right, this is my chance to show him what he's missing; I have exactly one hour to make myself beautiful. Okay, so shower, shave and then clothes and make-up, I think. I smile slightly as the prospect of getting ready for a posh evening out in Rome begins to dawn on me.

*   *   *

Stepping back and examining my reflection, I have to admit I'm impressed. This will show Dan; he's never seen me dressed up like this before and it's going to knock him off his feet. A low-backed version of the little black dress is set off by the elegant silver necklace and earrings, and the silver stilettos. My make-up looks surprisingly good for once and my hair has a slight wave in it, which I have decided to leave instead of straightening it. I mean, like they say, 'When in Rome' I should try out a new look, at least I think that's what the phrase means anyway.

Walking down to the lobby to meet Dan before heading to the restaurant, I try to look as nonchalant as possible, until I spot him through the other guests that are milling around. Good God, I did not think it was legal to look that hot. As soon as I get into power I shall pass a law declaring that all men, especially very pretty men, must always wear tuxedos or expensive well-made suits.

Realising that I had stopped dead while staring at him, I fake looking for something in my purse before stepping towards him.

I see him look up and his eyes are actually lighting up. Wow, Rome must really be magical, I didn't think I'd have this much of an effect. Composing myself I put my hand up to wave and smile as I grow closer to him, when someone knocks into me as they rush past. Just as I open my mouth to say something, I notice that Dan seems to have his tongue stuck down her throat. What the...?

"Oh right, sorry, Sophie, this is Chloe."

YOU HAVE GOT TO BE JOKING!

Chapter Four
Shoes solve all problems

Searching Chloe's face for signs of irritation and finding none, I decide to continue with my rant about public transport and the state of the tube stations in London at the moment compared to those here in Rome and other major European cities. Ten minutes later, I have finally run out of steam, and glancing up from my large glass of wine I see that she is still sitting alert and apparently listening to what I have been saying. God, this woman is relentless. Okay, time to get the attention away from me; I've run out of things to say and she really is starting to scare me now.

"So," I start sipping my drink again while I think of something to say, "how did you meet Dan?"

"Oh, it's a funny story really. It was a couple of years back when he was still freelancing, he was out in Kenya writing a piece on safari and there I was one day, my jeep stuck in the mud, my outfit ruined, and he rescued me." As she finishes this fascinating story, I am aware of the fixed grin across my face as her laugh cuts straight through me.

Luckily at this moment, Dan returns to the table carrying another bottle of wine – good, because if the evening carries on like this I'm going to need to forget it in the morning. Chloe's voice suddenly slices through my thoughts as she trills something about the two of us getting to know each other while hanging off Dan's arm like a lost puppy, and I have to make a conscious effort not to turn up my lip in distaste at her manner.

* * *

"It has nothing to do with the fact that I'm in love with Dan, I just don't like her because she's spoilt and rich," I say to Emily on the phone later that night, my words more than a little bit slurred. I've known her long enough now to know that she is shaking her head once again in disbelief over the phone.

"You really need to stop denying that you're jealous of her." Her voice sounds distant, but that might just be the fact that I have consumed my own body weight in expensive wine.

* * *

Dragging my suitcase off the conveyer belt, I feel like I've been away for over a week, and on possibly the worst and longest trip ever. I can't believe that my plans could have gone so wrong. I was really going to make him see me that night; why the hell did he bring his bloody girlfriend? I can't believe he did that. Just thinking about it is making me nearly shake with anger and humiliation. I need a drink. I need shopping. Okay, I need to go out before I get home and face telling the story, so I'll just do a bit of window-shopping and grab a couple of bottles of wine, and maybe some vodka.

* * *

"A stiletto heel is a thin, long heel found on some boots and shoes, usually for women you know! It got its name from the stiletto dagger, and I think the phrase was actually first recorded in the early 1930s." I am aware that the shop assistant is looking at me like I'm slightly demented, but I've had a traumatic few days so I carry on anyway.

"The heels of a stiletto may vary in length from 2.54cm up to 20.32cm, and some, known as kitten heels, are defined as having a diameter at the ground of less than 1cm."

Pausing for breath, I realise that there are now several people looking at me in an odd way, and that I may have sounded like a dictionary.

"So you see, I'm obligated to buy these shoes in order to carry on a legacy left to me and all women." I really should be a lawyer – my arguments are fantastic and I don't feel any guilt at all for buying these shoes. I mean, sure they may cost about the same as a deposit on a nice car, but just look at them: the way the silver catches the light as you strut up and down the smooth black satin, and the little diamonds on the slingback buckle are just so pretty. I mean, no normal woman could possibly resist;

plus, I really do need them to cheer me up.

Being careful to dispose of the ridiculously large shoebox, and carefully hiding the beautiful new additions to my wardrobe in my handbag – I knew there was a reason we always have handbags that are so damn big – I head home, skulking guiltily past the living room, and Emily, to hide them in the box under my bed for especially expensive purchases. Pushing the box back under my bed and pulling down the covers I breathe deeply, and then look around to double check that Emily hasn't seen me. Standing up with a smile of victory on my face – the first in a while – I switch on my computer and follow my stomach to the Pot Noodle in the cupboard and the vodka on the side. Stirring it slowly with my spoon, being careful not to splash boiling water all over my arms, I sit down next to Emily in the living room.

"I didn't hear you come in," she says, looking up at me as I smile at her through a mouthful of noodles.

"I, erm… thought you might be asleep so I was quiet," I reply, not really very convincingly.

"Why would I be sleeping, Soph?"

Oh crap, she's raising her eyebrows, she suspects, quickly… I need to throw her off the scent before she starts a search and finds out I have bought another pair of shoes rather than paying the electricity bill. My eighty-sixth pair of shoes.

"Oh, just because I saw Mr Stevens on the way in and he said that he heard some very strange noises coming from our flat last night. In fact, he said he was quite worried, thought someone might be hurt. So I just thought, after all that exercise, you might be tired and so, being the wonderful flatmate I am, I decided to be extra quiet coming in today just in case you were sleeping."

"He heard that!" she screams, her face flushing beetroot. Bloody hell I didn't expect that reaction, I didn't even see Mr Stevens, I must be psychic, oh quick think of something to say to make sure she stays completely off the scent.

"Well, short of having soundproofing put in and some heavy duty earplugs, there's no way he couldn't have heard it. His words, not mine." I smile to myself, as her face is growing steadily redder than I thought to be humanly possible.

"So, what are you up to tonight then?" Emily stutters, quickly steering the conversation away from her sex life, and I inwardly jump for joy – success!

"Oh, just some research on Tuscany ready for my article."

"When are you going?"

"End of the week, but I'm only there for two days so I'll be back Sunday night".

"This weekend?" she asks curiously. "You know that's tomorrow right?"

"Yes, of course I do. So it's Thursday today then?"

"Yes, it's Thursday, have you packed?"

"Well, sort of, I was actually going to finish tonight." Shit, okay I really need to buy a diary and keep track of my days more. How did I not realise that I was going away tomorrow? It doesn't matter, though, because I haven't really unpacked from Rome yet, so I'll take the smaller case and just take out the stilettos and the nice dresses from the Rome trip and take some shorts and T-shirts. It's fine, I'll just go and prepare now. I've been to Tuscany before so I don't need to do too much research, and it's only two days. That's only one suitcase and my hand luggage, if I pack lightly. So, reluctantly, I drag myself off the sofa and, walking into the hall, I open the cupboard and fight my way through its contents to find my blue suitcase – the only one that really goes with my planned traveling outfit. Honestly, there's a lot more to being a travel writer than meets the eye, you know; I mean, you have to always look the part, without looking quite like a tourist but still professional and business-like.

Sitting down in front of the mirror, I stare intently at my reflection, wondering why exactly it is that he chose her over me. Okay, so taking away the fact that she is extremely rich, maybe it's my roots? They aren't exactly looking great at the moment, but then again my hair was looking perfect when he asked her out. Maybe it's my teeth; I've been meaning to have a word with my dentist about some invisible braces. Last time I asked for them he said I was just being paranoid because my teeth were fine, and he didn't seem impressed at my offer of a small bribe. I mean honestly, it was only going to be a little present in exchange for a nicer smile. I still have four of those cappuccino machines stuffed in the hall cupboard, which I really need to get rid of before Emily finds them.

They were a great buy though, what a bargain! Two for the price of one. Only problem is, once I bought them I realised I didn't need four, and everyone I know seems to have one already, so they're actually harder to get rid of than I had thought. Plus I need the space in the bottom of the cupboard to put those new storage boxes I bought last week, which reminds me, I really need to go shopping to get some of those fab little trinket boxes and things to put in them.

Okay, back to the mirror. Turning back to face it I jump as Leona Lewis's voice starts exploding from beneath a pile of clothes on my bed. Oh bugger, that will be Dan calling about the meeting tomorrow morning, and I really didn't want to speak to him for a long time after the last few days. Rifling through the clothes, I send knickers flying all over the place as I grab for the flashing screen.

"Hello," I say, slightly out of breath, "Oh hello, Mum."

"Hi, sweetheart."

"You alright?"

"Oh yes, just at work and thought I'd give you a ring."

"Your boss annoying you then, is he?"

"He's such a bastard, Soph, silly pig-headed little man."

"Alright, Mum, calm down, he might hear you."

"I don't care any more."

"Yes you do, what about Sarah and Pat? You love working with them, don't you?"

"Well yes, but…"

"See! So what did you really ring about?"

"I was just wondering where you were off to next?"

"Italy, on Friday actually."

"That soon? Didn't you just get back from Rome? Why didn't you tell me?"

"Yes, I did just get back today but I lead a busy life, and I did tell you I was away nearly all week."

"No you didn't."

"Yes I did, last week when you were going on about taking Nan shopping."

"No, you were talking about going to Tuscany then."

45

"Yes – Italy!"

"Tuscany is in France, Sophie."

"No it's not, it's in Italy."

"No, it's in France, ask your father!"

"I bloody will and it's Italy! Who's the travel writer here?"

"That's not the point; besides, it sounds very French."

"No it doesn't, and like I'm going to believe you – you told me bruschetta was a type of cheese!"

"That was years ago."

"Still said it though, didn't you? What is that noise?"

"Head teacher telling off a kid."

"Bloody hell, what did the kid do, shoot someone?"

"No, not exactly. I've got to go, darling, I'll give you a ring tonight when I'm on my way home."

"Ring me when you *get* home, not on your *way* home. You can never hear a word I'm saying when you have me on speaker phone and I always end up shouting to thin air."

"Okay then, I'll speak to you later."

"Bye."

"Bye, love you!"

"Love you, speak to you later."

Putting down the phone I smile to myself as I get up, wrapping myself in a big stripy bath towel, and head towards the bathroom. Closing the door, I turn on the taps and start to run a bath, pouring in some of those new relaxing bath salts I got in Mark's and Spencer the other day. I light a few scented candles and quickly run out and back to my room to grab my cucumber facemask and my music. Stepping into the warm water, I sink down, placing the mask over my eyes and flicking on a Snow

Patrol album, determined to relax.

* * *

So okay, it's taken me two hours, but I think I'm finally finished packing and I've really cut down this time – only four pairs of shoes. I know it's not exactly leaving much room for wardrobe disasters, but Dan will kill me and bury me in a shallow grave if I don't cut down. His words not mine. The song 'Colourblind' starts playing in the background and I hum along for a couple of seconds. Where is that music coming from? Oh shit, it's my phone, maybe I shouldn't change my ringtone so much, then I might actually realise my phone is ringing! Where did I put it? Oh how did it get inside my suitcase? Now I'm going to have to refold that whole top part, damn!

"Hi, Dad."

"Hi. You rang me earlier?"

"Did I? Oh yeah, I was just going to ask if I could borrow a little bit of money so that I can get to the airport tomorrow." Holding my breath, I wait for his answer.

"No."

"What? But you promised me some money for my shopping the other week and you never gave it to me." I am suddenly aware that my voice has taken on its whiny tone.

"I'm not funding your shopping any more, Sophie."

"But I haven't bought anything in ages."

"So why did another three hundred pounds come out of your account yesterday then?"

"That was for the new throws for the living room seats. I had to buy those, the other ones were horrible!"

"You only bought them two months ago!"

"Well yes, but they were looking really old already and they just don't match anything else in the room any more." Oops, now he's going to know I bought a whole load of new furniture too. Bugger!

"I'm not discussing it, Sophie, it's time to grow up and be responsible."

"Fine, but I already told you I haven't bought anything."

"Bye, Sophie."

"Bye." Hanging up the phone I feel automatically guilty for getting angry, but I can't really help it when I have to buy, I just have to buy; but I suppose they are kind of right in a way, just a tiny bit. But I resent the growing up bit completely. I am so grown-up – I live on my own, I pay all my bills, and my rent, I travel the world, I have adult relationships – well, at least I would if the opportunity ever decided to arise – I am very grown-up! I mean, to be fair there is the occasional time that they have paid my Telewest bills, but the Internet is a vital part of my work and I need it for research, so I had no choice but to ask them for help with that, and the Oyster card was a birthday present, sort of, so I didn't actually ask for that. Damn it, I really feel guilty now. Bloody parents, honestly. Picking up my phone again, I wait for my dad to answer.

"Hello."

"Hi, Dad," I say in my most apologetic voice.

"What now?" he still sounds quite irritated. I'll have to tackle this one very carefully.

"Oh, nothing, I just wanted to say thank you."

"What for?"

"Oh, erm, you know… the… stuff." I hate grovelling. Plus if I apologise too much then he'll just think I want something else.

"That's okay."

Phew, well at least he sounds less annoyed, almost amused actually, which is probably at my stuttering attempt at an apology, but I'll take it, it's better than angry.

"So…" I struggle for a change of subject before things get awkward, "doing anything interesting today?"

"Well, it's a Thursday, so I'm working at the moment." Now he sounds bewildered and amused.

"Of course, I knew that, I meant tonight." I really need to get a watch that is really a mini calendar or something. That's a good idea actually. I must remember to put it on my list of things to invent.

"No, not really, just badminton."

"Oh cool, well, I'll leave you to it then. I'll probably see you when I get back from Tuscany. Also, by the way, where do you think Tuscany is, Dad?"

"Italy. Soph, you should know that seeing as you are going there, and you're a travel writer!"

"Course I know, Dad, you just tell Mum that, and tell her that I said 'I told her so'."

"Rightio then, see you soon, bye," and with that he is gone, and I feel a lot better – not the best apology in the world I'll admit, but hopefully it'll do the trick for now. Besides, I'll buy them a nice present when I'm away, that'll smooth things over. Turning back to the computer screen I scroll through the page that I have up idly, while half listening to the TV in the background.

Wow, that throw is beautiful, and it has matching curtains and they're half price. I just have to get them, I've been looking for a new set for years, well okay months, but still, my home is my workplace half of the time so I have to have a good environment. Plus these curtains just scream grown-up, which is exactly what they told me to be, so they technically told me to buy them. So, with a swift click of my finger on the mouse they are on the way from New York, and swinging round on my chair I jump up and head out to make myself a victory coffee; after all, I did just very convincingly win the argument for the curtains against my parents, it's just a pity they weren't here to listen to it and eat their words. Shit that hurt, bloody stool; ever since I bought it I've had nothing but pain. It cost me a fortune and it's impossible to sit on, and every time I enter the kitchen I stub my toe on its stupid, shiny, pointy metal leg thing!

Heading back into my room, complete with a couple of biscuits I found in the back of the cupboard, I stare in dismay at the pile of clothes hanging out of my suitcase. Time to repack and then I should probably sleep – I do have to be up at four a.m. to get the taxi to the airport.

Sitting down exhausted after a further hour of repacking, I had to give myself a pat on the back for managing to fit in my Gucci raincoat – it is a bit bulky, but after sitting on the case several times and removing most of the skin from my fingers, I closed it.

Dragging my laptop onto the bed with me I switch on the TV and flick around until I find a Channel 4 documentary about a girl born with eight limbs, and sit back against my pillows. Tapping away for twenty minutes to try and find information and facts to save me time when I write my article proves a little fruitless, and I write up a little of my article on Rome, leaning back to read over the paragraph I have written. Eventually, I give up and decide that I have done enough for now, so I turn off the computer. God it's quiet when that's switched off, I'm not sure it's supposed to be that loud – think I'll get it checked out when I get home next week.

* * *

Blindly reaching for my phone as my alarm, Justin Timberlake's 'My Love', blares out, I stretch out and whimper slightly with the pain of being woken up this early. I swear I've only been asleep for ten minutes, and I think my eyes may actually be sealed shut. Maybe rubbing them will help, oh shit! No, that just hurts. A lot! Okay, so shower, that will wake me up.

Shivering slightly as I step out of the shower into the cold morning air, I rush through to the kitchen and switch on the kettle as I get myself some cereal and a cup of strong black coffee. Putting on the TV – there is never anything good on at four o'clock in the morning, I should write to someone about that – I switch on the DVD player and the theme tune of 'Boston Legal' erupts from the speakers as I pull my hair back and start putting on my make-up. Four-thirty, that's okay, I still have fifteen minutes to double check I've got everything I need before the taxi gets here.

As my phone vibrates, I put the final kisses on the note I had just written to Emily on the whiteboard that hangs in our hallway, grab my case and handbag and step into the morning air. Well, that is after I nearly fall down the three flights of stairs and emerge sweating slightly, just as the cab is about to pull away, and then I get my heel caught in a crack in the pavement and nearly break it. Settling down in the back of the cab again, after we had already got ten minutes down the road and I remembered that I had left the tickets at home forcing us to race back to the flat to get them, I reach for my phone and search for Dan's number.

"Dan Shorely."

God, he sounds sexy when he answers the phone, and quite tired too actually. Could it be that I'm more awake and with it than he is?

"Hey, Dan, it's me, just thought I'd let you know I'm on the way to the airport."

"Why?"

"Because we're going to Tuscany today," – and he calls me forgetful!

"But it's five in the morning, Sophie, the flight's not until eleven!"

"Yes exactly, which means that we have to be there to check in at nine latest and I want to get some shopping in before that – you can never be too early."

"Jesus, Sophie, you're telling me that you are on your way to the airport four hours early so that you can do some shopping?"

"Yes." Why had he sounded so incredulous?

52

"You have a problem, Sophie, I'll see you later!"

"Ok. Bye." Hanging up the phone I catch a glimpse of the cab driver smirking at me in the mirror and shoot him a bit of a scowl before turning my gaze to the window. Okay, so technically I may have misread the time on the tickets and thought that the flight was at nine, but it's fine, it just means I can buy a good book and settle down on a nice seat somewhere, and I may even get some more notes written.

Chapter Five
Mixed signals

Wow, I think coffee is needed before I do anything else or I may fall asleep on the spot. I wish they had a special early check-in for people who liked to be early for a little shopping. This suitcase is bloody heavy, and it's not my fault if I trip up any more people. I refuse to take responsibility for it even if they are old and a little bit blind, they should be more careful about looking where they are going. Ah Starbucks, that will cheer me up a bit. I might buy a cookie too, seeing as when I'm with Dan I have to be on my best behavior and eat bugger all. It's such a pain, especially when we go to places that are famous for beautiful food. But like they say, there's no pain without gain, or is that the other way round? Anyway, judging by the disaster that was Rome, I need to step up my game, or lose half my body weight, and get rich quick!

Glancing at my watch I sigh heavily – still only half past six. I can't even check in yet and I've been round all the shops on this side already – the good ones are all on the other side. Oh well, if the flight's at eleven that means I can check in at nine, which means I've only got to wait for Dan for another TWO AND A HALF HOURS! Oh great, might as well do some writing then, or I could nip back into WH Smith and buy that book I was looking at. I mean, it might not be in the shops on the other side of security, plus this man next to me smells quite strongly of something I can't exactly put my finger on, and if he nods off again and his head touches my shoulder, I'm afraid the smell will rub off on me.

So hopping up and promptly sitting back down, as I find my hand still attached to my suitcase. That hurt. Okay, so off on another swerving trip to the bookshop and maybe some sweets for the plane. Wandering past the magazine rack, I automatically pick up a copy of the magazine I work for and flick straight to my article on Portugal from our trip last month. Scanning through, I can't find… The bloody cheek of the woman, she took out the best bit again! Throwing the glossy mag back down on the shelf, I head back out to wait for Dan.

Half past eight and no sign of Dan. Where the bloody hell is he? He's not usually late, I am! Well the tables have turned today, and not just because I got the wrong flight times and was too stubborn to admit it and ended up here ridiculously early instead of getting a few extra hours sleep. Now, do I wait here like a lemon or do I queue up on my own like a lemon and get us good seats? I think I'll queue; he might even be pleased that I saved him most of the queuing bit if he hurries and gets here before

I've already checked in. Seriously, where is he! There are only two people left in front of me now. Standing on my tippie toes – not an easy thing to do in heels – I peer around the crowded airport to try and spy a well-dressed, good-looking man. Wow, there are a lot of them here, maybe I've been searching for a man in the wrong place, they seem to have all gathered here. Huh, who would have guessed?

"Sophie."

Was that someone calling my name or am I more sleep-deprived than usual today? Looking around, though, I can see his perfectly groomed head bobbing towards me rather rapidly. Just like him to miss the boring queuing bit.

"Over here," I call out to him, motioning for him to hurry up as I try to delay walking up to the counter for as long as possible, ignoring the impatient tutting behind me.

"Sorry I'm late," he announces breathlessly as he reaches my side, "I got caught up saying goodbye to Chloe."

Eww, I don't want to know that.

"Oh that's fine," I say, trying to find a balance between nonchalance and sarcasm.

"So, did you have enough time to get all that shopping in then?"

"Passports please," chips in the woman with… wow, that really is an extraordinarily large and oddly shaped nose.

"Yes, thank you," I reply quickly, as I hand over my passport and other documents.

"Well I don't see as many bags as usual," he mocks, looking down.

Crap, I can't admit that I just got the times wrong, and now

56

that bloody woman's talking again and I can't concentrate.

"Did anyone give you anything to carry on board?"

"What? Oh erm, yes."

"Sophie, did you even hear what she just said?"

"Yes, of course I did, she asked if we packed the cases ourselves." Honestly, I know the order of questions like the back of my hand.

"No she didn't."

"What?"

"I asked if anyone had given you anything to take on board."

"Oh sorry, I misheard you, no… no one gave me anything." Who does she think she is changing the order of the bloody questions? That's like changing the order of the Commandments! I can feel my face flushing as I try and hurry through the rest of the process as quickly as possible. This is not shaping up to be the best of days so far.

"So shall we go through then?" I say, walking away speedily from the line of slightly impatient people whom I had just held up.

"Well, I was going to look for a book first."

"You can get that on the other side, come on, I'm starving and I want some breakfast."

"Why didn't you get some before I got here?"

"Because all the nice restaurants are on the other side."

"On the other side? You sound like you're talking about going to heaven or something."

"Shut up, it's been a long morning."

"Okay, well let's go then, and please remember not to

mention bombs around security, they tend to be a bit stricter than the checking-in women, and I am not rescuing you from a large woman with a pair of rubber gloves."

"Ha, bloody, ha, it was an accident. How was I to know she was going to change the order of the questions? I mean, it shouldn't be allowed," I say slightly shamefacedly, trying to regain my dignity and at the same time picturing that unpleasant lady with the gloves.

* * *

I love travelling, mainly because it means for each new place you go it is imperative to have a new and fitting outfit. Which means a whole wardrobe dedicated to clothes purely for travelling; but all that said, even I can't find a good reason to come home one day and go straight back to the same bloody country the next. Not my fault though, Dan arranged it. Actually, thinking about it, if we had gone straight on to Tuscany, Chloe would have probably joined us for a further two torturous days. I've got my work cut out for me as well since I'm not going to look nearly as glamorous as I did in Rome, and I have a feeling Chloe is the sort of person who looks fantastic in a bin bag, whereas I, on the other hand, can be dressed in Armani and still look like a bin bag. None of that matters, however, because I am guaranteed Dan to myself this time as Chloe had to fly home to go too some event, not that I care or am the slightest bit peeved that she ruined my private jet ride home. I'm just glad that she won't be there this time, although part of me would find it hilarious to see her in a youth hostel. But anyway where was I? Oh yes all this means that not only do I get him all to myself, I can start again and make sure that the wheels are set in motion.

* * *

I daydream my way through the security, coming to briefly when I get told to remove my shoes and struggle for about ten minutes with the little buckles. Stupid shoes – they do look good though, and they were such a bargain. Only cost me thirty-five down from seventy – I know, incredible! I wasn't even looking for shoes at the time. Actually, I was supposed to be finding out information on the different prices for trips to Greece from the travel agents and there they were, just sitting in Topshop! Well, that is to say… they were sitting in the sale section in the back corner hidden by two pairs of boots; but I didn't mean to go in there, I sort of got dragged in by the crowd that was heading that way.

Sitting down, I suddenly realise that I have been ushered past all the shops and straight into the restaurant; he really is good at catching me off guard like that and steering me past the places I would have gone into. Looking up, I notice he is sitting opposite me, his phone out as usual, and it suddenly strikes me that this is almost like a date – the first such occasion in a very long time – and it is now up to me to take full advantage of this situation.

The waiter comes over to take our drinks order, and looking across at the bar, I see a couple has just walked in wearing awful matching jumpers. Oh dear, I really should go and tell them that they just look so wrong, but it's not my place to save every person I see from their fashion disasters. Scanning across the rest of the restaurant, I can see a variety of people dotted around. I love people watching, it keeps me entertained for hours, especially when Dan sits there with his bloody phone out. Now that's a well-dressed man, in fact he rivals Sam in that department; his dark hair seems to be perfectly placed too. Turn around, turn around so I can see what you look like. Wow, he's beautiful too, that's just not fair. Oh my God, he's coming this way, it's like something out of a movie, love at first sight – these shoes really do work.

"Dan, is that you?" His voice was so deep and sexy it was possibly even better than Vin Diesel's. There would be no need for me to watch 'Triple X' again because I'd be living with that sexy voice. Hang on a minute, did he just say Dan?

"James, how are you? It's been years!"

"Fine! Actually, I'm directing now."

"Really, how's that going for you?"

Is it just me, or can I detect a slight note of distaste in Dan's tone?

"Great, actually I'm off to LA to shoot a film."

I'm not really listening to what he's saying, although everything he does is making me fall deeper, and as I stare into his stunningly bright-green eyes I am becoming increasingly annoyed at Dan for not introducing me, and for being mean to my future husband.

"So anyway, what are you up to these days, still doing your little writing thing?"

Hang on a minute, did he just belittle my career? That bastard!

"Yes actually, James, and it's going well thank you. This is my work partner, Sophie Farrier." His voice is tight and his jaw is set and now I'm pissed off with this James person for ruining my imaginary date with Dan and for slagging off my career. But I'm nothing if not professional, so I'll have to be nice to the bastard.

"Hello, Sophie." Okay, just don't look into his eyes. Oh, his teeth are perfect, and his mouth… just look down. Wow, okay, best just to look at something that isn't him then.

"Hi," I say in my most nonchalant way. "I suppose you should be getting on then. I wouldn't like to think our little writing thing would get in the way of your directing." Okay, so maybe that was a little on the bitchy side rather than the professional, but it started well. Glancing at Dan I can see a flicker of humour cross his face. Then, looking back at James, I can see the same in his; hang on a minute, he's not supposed to find that funny.

"I suppose I should be going then, it was nice to meet you, Sophie, and I look forward to reading some of your work. Hope I see you soon. Bye, Dan."

"See you."

"Bye then, good luck in America, don't get sunburned."

Did he just wink at me? How dare he! I can't believe he just winked at me, the bloody cheek. Does that mean he likes me? Amazing what this new mascara can do!

"So," I say, trying to stay calm at the fact that I seem to have impressed Dan and the hot stranger – a good start to this trip after all, I think. "The full English breakfast for both us?"

"I think that would be a fitting celebration for your victory," he laughs.

"Victory?"

"Yeah, well you managed to shut him up, which is something I was never good at."

"It's a gift I have you know."

"Yeah I know!"

"So, how do you know him anyway?"

"Went to uni with him."

"So, is he single then?" I press, trying to sound uninterested.

"I don't know, but he's not for you."

"Oh really, and why is that then? What, he's too posh and rich for me?"

"Well there is that, but seriously, you can do better."

"What?"

"Soph, you can do better, trust me! So, hash browns or toast then?"

I flush slightly as I realise that I just had a moment with Dan. I really think this is going to be the trip to steal him away from Chloe.

Chapter Six
Sunburn and Chardonnay

This is more like what I'm used to – away from the posh hotel in Rome, sweating it up in a youth hostel without air conditioning and my hair a frizzy mess because I forgot my adapter for the straighteners. Yet I can't stop smiling, even though it's eight in the morning on a Saturday, my legs are aching from yesterday's trekking up and down the mountains that they call hills here, half my body is covered with mosquito bites and I have the headache from hell after polishing off that bottle of wine last night – or was it two, who knows? But what is important for me to remember is that, despite all this, I have been on a roll with Dan. Ever since my little outburst in the restaurant at the airport he seems to have seen me in a new light, which can only be good for me, but, however, I do need to set the wheels in motion and the idea planted in his head before he gets home to Chloe.

I get out of my, well I guess it's supposed to be a bed, and wander down the hall to jump in the shower for some relief. The water trickles over my body cooling it down and the stickiness is replaced by that lovely clean feeling. It lasts for about all of twenty seconds, and as soon as I step out of the shower I'm practically sweating again. Heading back to my room, I throw on a vest top and a pair of shorts – colour coordinated of course – and tie my hair back. Of course I am never to be seen without make-up, so, taking the weather into consideration, it's my usual hot country combination of tinted foundation, a bit of bronzer, waterproof mascara (very important that bit – I remember that first time I went to Greece and didn't use waterproof mascara, and by mid-morning I looked like a panda!) and lip gloss. It gives the effect of someone who looks after their appearance but doesn't go over the top, and it's still comfortable.

Setting off we have a 'short' two-hour minibus journey to the bottom of another huge mountain. After a further three hours I am a little over halfway up, panting, my legs shaking from the strain of walking uphill for so long, and I give in and sit on a rock. Dan has practically reached the top already and looks like he is laughing at me, although to be honest he is so far away that the dot I think is him could well be a sheep. Unzipping my backpack, I yank out my water and my phone and dial Ruth's number.

"Hello."

"Ruth, save me," I say, being completely serious, seeing as I don't think my poor blistered feet will manage to get me home.

"Sophie, where the hell are you? Save you from what?" she

sounds completely bewildered.

"I'm halfway up a mountain in the middle of Italy, and I need you to save me from, well, from the mountain," I say, leaning back against another rock.

"And how am I supposed to do that?" she laughs at me.

"I don't know, send a helicopter," I plead.

"I think you might just have to brave it I'm afraid, darling."

"But…"

"Sorry, Soph, I have to go, I've got a fitting for my dress in half an hour. See you soon, bye."

"Bye," I reply meekly, but she has already gone. Well, she was a great help, honestly.

* * *

Seriously, never again! I am making a declaration now that I will never again walk up a bloody Italian mountain. I don't think I've ever had so many blisters in my life, and I completely forgot suncream this morning so my shoulders are now literally glow-in-the-dark red.

"Right, okay, so shall we have a drink then?" Dan shouts back, as I am now practically crawling the last few metres back to the hotel. I nod a response, too tired to respond with words.

"Over here, Soph," he gestures, as I hobble onto the little veranda and towards the table, which already has an ice bucket and bottle of wine sitting on it. God, I love this man.

"Thanks," I sigh, taking a huge gulp of the best-tasting red wine ever, and look up at him as he smiles at me, shaking his head.

"What?" I say. What have I done now? I bet I have bloody mud on my face or something.

"Nothing, you just make me laugh that's all."

What's that supposed to mean then?

"I don't understand," I question him, slightly worried about what I have done. I don't relish another month of photos on the noticeboard at work.

"It's nothing bad, I just mean you're a fun person to be around."

He's making my legs go shaky again, or maybe that's just because my muscles have all exploded from trying to get up that mountain. I just smile at him with a puzzled expression on my face and then take another gulp of wine, before getting distracted by a couple of local people arguing on the road below.

"They seem to be getting into it a bit," I comment as I stare at them. Looking over at them he watches for a couple of minutes before chuckling.

"What?"

"They're arguing over their pets."

"Sorry what?" I ask again, totally confused.

"Apparently, the bloke's dog has been terrorising the woman's cat," he laughs.

"How do you know that?"

"That's what she just said."

"But you don't speak Spanish," I say incredulously.

"I know…" he says, looking at me with that amused twinkle in his eye, "but I do speak Italian."

"Since when?" I ask, ignoring the fact that I may have got the languages mixed up again.

"Since school."

"Oh…" Now that he mentions it I do have a vague recollection of a similar conversation taking place in Rome the other day.

"Do you never listen to anything I say?" he asks with what might be real hurt in his voice, but is probably just him mocking me as usual.

"Yes, of course I do, I was only joking. I remember you telling me the other day." I think I got away with that – good recovery, Sophie, I think I'll have another glass of wine to celebrate.

"Yeah right," he says smiling, making my heart flutter ever so slightly.

"So, what are they saying now?" I say, changing the subject again.

"Let me listen a minute," he says, concentrating on straining to listen to the argument, and I pour another glass of wine and let its cold fruitiness soothe my throat and aching limbs.

"Oh my God," he says with an astounded look on his face, as he begins to laugh uncontrollably.

"What?" I say, nearly spitting out a mouthful of wine in my hurry to get the word out.

"I can't believe he just said that."

"What?" I say again impatiently. I hate it when people do this. It's like when they say, I have a massive secret, and you ask them what it is, and then they say, oh, I can't tell you. I hate that.

"He actually just said, well your cat started it," he manages through his laughter.

"No, you're winding me up," I giggle.

"No seriously, that's what he said."

67

"I don't believe you, you must have translated it wrongly," I say again, beginning to laugh at him laughing – I've never seen him this amused in my life. I pour him another glass of wine and we sit talking and laughing for a good few hours, until he finally says its time for us to go and pack our stuff up and shower.

* * *

It's half past nine and we are leaving in the morning. So, after packing my stuff, I am sitting on the edge of the bed with my towel wrapped around me, trying to put aftersun on my very sore shoulders, when a knock at the door startles me and I spill half the bottle. Dan pokes his head round the door and I can see him wince when he sees my shoulders.

"Jesus, Sophie, that's worse than the time you got burnt in Mexico."

"I know," I almost wail, "it's killing!"

"Here, let me put that stuff on, you'll never reach."

"Okay." I give him the bottle and he kneels behind me and starts to gently rub it in. Oh fuck, this is it. This is the moment I've been waiting for to make him start to see that I am the one he should be with, not little-miss-stuck-up idiot-face. But what do I do? Crap, I have no idea what to do next.

"Thanks," I say, trying to sound sexy.

"That any better?" he says as if he's finished, but leaving his hands on my shoulders he continues to massage them gently.

"Oh wow, yeah, that feels really good." Did I actually just say that? Shit, I did, and now he's laughing. Well that's just great, Sophie, you opened your big mouth again and ruined everything. But hang on a second, he hasn't stopped, why hasn't he stopped?

"So…" he starts almost awkwardly, "I've… I've had a good trip with you here."

"What's that supposed to mean? It's usually bloody awful." I feign hurt in my voice.

"No, I didn't… you know what I mean, we just seem to have had more time to talk."

"Maybe that's because you weren't on the phone to bloody Chloe every five minutes," I mutter under my breath.

"You're right."

"Sorry, I…" Shit, he wasn't supposed to hear that, I must really work on my muttering quietly skills.

"No, you're right. Listen, I've been spending too much time with her recently and I, well I'm going to try and…" He is interrupted when his phone rings suddenly and the second of tension between us as his eyes meet mine is incredible – quite literally the stuff from my dreams. Except instead of kissing me like he would in my dream, he breaks his gaze and looks at the display on his phone before standing up.

"I'd better take this." He looks at me for a second before flipping the phone open and turning to leave the room.

"Hi baby. How are you? Yes, I miss you too…"

I hate men. They say we are the fickle ones, are you kidding? I fall backwards onto the thin mattress, crying out in pain as I remember my shoulders are on fire.

Chapter Seven
Rehearsal dinners, rehearsal dates

Taking one last look in the mirror, I back away from it and, picking up my bag, totter into the hall, calling out for Emily to hurry up. I can't believe that I'm on my way to my little brother's wedding rehearsal dinner. It's not bloody fair – the whole order of everything has been messed up. I mean, it makes sense that I should get married before him. He's still a baby, twenty-two for God's sake! He shouldn't even be considering marriage yet, it's just ridiculous.

"You still brooding over the fact that Harry's getting married before you?" Emily laughs behind me as I examine myself in the hall mirror this time.

"It's not fair, Em! He should be at my wedding first." I screw my face up as I say this and reapply my lipstick for the thirteenth time.

"Get over it, you idiot, he'll still be your little brother when you get married, won't he?"

"Well yeah, but he will have a wife!"

"So…"

"So, it will just be weird." Honestly, she doesn't understand a word I'm saying half the time.

"You know you're just being ridiculous, right?"

"Am not."

"Yes, you are."

"Whatever." A little support in my troubled times wouldn't go amiss. "Besides, what with Ruth getting married too, I just feel a bit left out."

"You're crazy, you know that?"

"No, I'm not."

"Yes, you are. Left out? You're Ruth's maid of honour!"

"Well yeah, I know, but…"

"But what? Stop moaning."

Moaning! I was not moaning. Honestly!

"Where's Sam? The cab will be here any minute."

"Relax, Soph, he's just parking his car, then he'll be up."

"Oh right, okay then. Do you think this top goes?"

"Yes, you look great."

"I don't know, I think I'll go change."

"Into what?"

"That top I bought the other day."

"What top?"

"Oh you know, the pink satin vest top with bits round the top." Oops! I forgot I hadn't told her about that particular buy.

"Are you telling me you bought a top exactly the same as the

71

one you are wearing now in a different colour?"

I actually bought it in four different colours but I don't think I'll mention that now.

"Maybe," is my feeble reply. A change of subject is needed quick. "The taxi should be here by now."

"I thought you were changing?"

I hate it when she raises her eyebrows at me like that.

"Well, I was going to keep this on so I don't have to rethink my shoes too. Why, do you think I need to change?"

"No! I already said you look fine!"

Fine! Jesus, does that woman know how to make a girl paranoid or what? Then Sam knocks on the door and, taking a last glimpse in the mirror, I add a powder compact to my already bulging clutch bag and tear myself away.

Oh my God, Sam looks breathtaking. I mean, I knew the man could dress but wow, it's all I can do not to dribble. Watching as he greets her with a kiss, I can't help thinking that it would probably be illegal for them to reproduce, simply because their children would just be too good looking. Pulling the door shut behind me, the three of us start to walk down to the waiting taxi.

"Hello, Sophie, you look lovely," Sam says, as we are halfway down the two flights of stairs.

"Thanks." I'm blushing, I can't believe it, that girl is so lucky. I mean, I know he's a bit boring and everything, but still, he certainly knows the right things to say. I might get him to teach Em that trick so she doesn't panic me with a 'you look fine' at the last minute.

As I sit in the cab I feel suddenly emotional. In a few minutes

I'll be sitting at a table with my brother and the woman he will be marrying in two months time. The dinner is being held at Down Hall, an old country house, which is all a bit posh for me really but it's not that far away and I suppose sets the tone for the actual wedding, which, from what I've heard, is going to be amazing. Then again her family is loaded from what I can gather, and I guess if you can afford it, why not?

Pulling up outside the old building, I feel slightly in awe as I do with any old or expensive looking building and I suddenly feel underdressed. I knew I should have changed my top. It seems dead quiet outside. Mind you, it is October so it would make sense that everyone is already inside out of the elements. Picking my way across the gravel in my beautiful new four-inch stilettos – by far the best part of my outfit today – I look like a complete misfit. In front of me, Emily and Sam are walking arm-in-arm looking like they totally belong there and I'm stumbling all over the shop, trying desperately to stay on my feet. Okay, actually not staying on my feet at all really.

Stepping onto a particularly slippery bit of gravel I suddenly feel myself pitching forward, and just as I'm about to hit the floor, completely embarrass myself and ladder my tights, strong arms grab me swiftly from behind and haul me upwards. Wow, whoever it is must be really strong to haul me anywhere, especially away from gravity! Turning around to get a look at my saviour, I'm so shocked I nearly fall flat on my arse again, and I think I would have done if he wasn't still holding onto me.

"It's you!" I say in a very shocked and shaky voice.

"It's me," he replies in his deep sexy voice, an amused look spreading across his face.

"It's James, right?" I say, still standing really close to him. Oh my God, oh my God, it's the really hot bloke from the airport.

"Yeah that's right, so you remember me then?"

"Yeah, I guess I do." I know I was supposed to be mad at him, but when I'm this close to someone this hot it's hard to remember why.

"So, shall we go inside then, Sophie? It's a bit cold out here."

"Oh, erm, yes," I stutter. Bloody hell, Sophie, keep it together. "So what are you doing here anyway?" I try steadying my voice so I sound slightly more sane.

"Oh, I'm a friend of Jennifer, the bride. You?" His voice is so God damn sexy I can barely concentrate on what he is saying.

"The groom is my little brother," I reply as nonchalantly as possible.

"Well there you go then, it's a small world," he mutters as we enter the vast entrance hall.

I can't help gaping around like a goldfish; it honestly doesn't matter how many new places I go to or beautiful buildings I see, every one still gives me that same goose-pimply feeling on the back of my neck.

"Sweetie, darling, over here," my mum's voice comes trilling over everyone's heads. I really need to talk to her about the fact that she is beginning to morph into that woman from 'Absolutely Fabulous'.

"Hi, Mum," I say, as she comes trotting over.

"You're late, I was beginning to think you'd got lost or something. And who is this?" She has stopped paying attention to me and is now staring at James, who is smiling back at her.

74

"Hello, Mrs Farrier, I'm James." He's so polite, holding out his hand to her as she gawps at him even more obviously than me – so that's where I get it from.

"So, Mum," I interject quickly, "where's Dad?"

"Oh, he's over there with Harry and Jennifer," she says, coming to and suddenly bustling around again, before running off to talk to someone else who had just arrived.

"Well then," James smiles at me, and it's all I can do to stop my legs collapsing beneath me, "shall we go and say hello to the bride-and-groom-to-be?"

"Oh yes, I suppose we should," I say, suddenly remembering why we were here. "Hey, little brother," I say as I approach him. Bloody hell, he just gave me a kiss on the cheek. I think that's the most affection he's shown me in the last twenty years.

"Hello, Soph, how are you?" As he speaks to me I notice how well spoken he is and how deep his voice is. I could hardly believe that this man was my little brother. This used to be the little boy that had always reached my waist and relied on me to look after and protect him. He had always been the crybaby of the house, someone who needed looking after, and I suppose I just assumed he would always be there, but somewhere along the line I lost touch and now before me stood someone I didn't even know! Not that it was easy to get to know him – he was probably the most private person in the world. I still thought of him as a little boy and when I found out he was going to get married, well, I think that was the closest I've ever been to passing out. Hang on a minute, did he just greet James as a mate? How the bloody hell did he keep him a secret from me? I'll quiz him later.

*　*　*

It's now about half one in the morning, and sitting on the edge of my bed while I take off my shoes I am still musing over the evening I just had. Men are so bloody confusing. First, he completely blanks me and belittles my career, and then, four weeks later, he rescues me from falling over and is a complete gentleman in every way. Plus he acted like he wanted to be talking to me, so now I don't know what to do! Not that it matters I guess, because he's flying back to LA tomorrow morning and I'm back to work with Dan. Rubbing my feet for a couple of minutes, I continue to ponder my situation. Okay, so it's not really a situation, it's just a small dilemma in my head which I seem to have created. In my little fantasy world I need to pick a man, whereas in reality it is more a case of just picking one of them to focus more of my attention on and fantasise about more. It may be sad, but come on, it's as close as I am going to get at the moment. Besides, if I pick one of them to fancy more, then I can come up with a better plan for catching that one. God that makes them sound like fish or something, but still, it makes sense in my head anyway.

Slumping back onto my pillows, still half-dressed, I spend a couple of minutes weighing up the pros and cons of the two men before I fall asleep.

*　*　*

Shit! I forgot to take my make-up off again last night and now there are nice big black eyeliner stains on my pillows, and they were new as well, cost a bloody fortune, damn. Mind you, I did see that lovely new bed set in Bhs the other day; maybe I could nip there on my lunch break today. Dragging myself out of bed, I head for the shower and, standing under the warm water, I try and wake myself up, but it's not working that well and I still feel like I've only had an hour's sleep as I dry myself and get dressed. Opening my wardrobe, I let my eyes wander across all my clothes; well at least all the ones I could actually fit in, eventually settling on a pair of long black jeans, a white shirt and a pair of patent black kitten heels. The train is absolutely packed as usual but there's no way I could be bothered to drive everyday, especially with that bloody congestion charge, so I have to settle for being a sardine for twenty minutes every morning. Oh my God, somebody just trod on my shoe, the cheek of it, they've marked it! OH MY GOD, that is so annoying, I bet it was somebody wearing really ugly shoes as well! I feel like I should set up a little stand on the train one day so that I can explain to these people the importance of nice shoes, and the danger they face when they step on mine.

Chapter Eight
Meeting the GMTV crew

Opening my eyes blearily, I throw my arm out, trying to make my phone stop screaming at me to get up. What is the time? Five a.m. What the bloody hell did I set it for that time for? Oh crap, I remember... today's the day of my big break, my first television experience, and I get to meet Ben Shepherd – and between you and me I'm liking how Ben is turning himself out recently; I'd go so far as to say he was looking bloody sexy. Maybe I could get him to fall for me and then this whole Dan and James thing would completely disappear.

Right then, shower first; no wait, eyebrows, legs and bikini line first (you never know what might happen – I don't want to be that woman who collapsed on live TV and had to be resuscitated while the whole of Britain was laughing at my hairy legs and my hairy bits sticking out from my knickers, do I!).

Switching on my computer I trawl through the programs until I find my 'getting ready for work' playlist and start to hum along while I wander round my room looking for the best light in which to pluck my eyebrows to perfection. Walking backwards to keep the light I had found, I trip against a pile of clothes and shoes and fall backwards into the big whirring bottom bit of my computer – I think it's called a hard drive – and simultaneously manage to break the whole bloody machine. Now I have a massive graze down my thigh, which is shocking because now I definitely can't wear the skirt I was going to wear, which throws out my whole wardrobe for the day… SHIT!

Never mind, I have a couple of hours to sort that out later, I'll just concentrate on the rest of the showering preparations and get back to wardrobe choices later. Twenty minutes later and I have finally managed to pluck my eyebrows into a reasonable shape, one that doesn't look like I am permanently shocked by what is being said to me. I have also successfully removed all the hair from my legs and bikini line, except one little stubborn tuft on my knee that I have to remember to shave once I get in the shower. Wandering into the bathroom I try to be as quiet as possible so as not to wake up Emily and incur the wrath that would follow with her early-morning self. Not saying that she doesn't like mornings or anything, but I wouldn't like to see what the person who woke her up would look like after she had finished with them.

Checking the time as I enter my room, complete with a coffee and having only made a small puddle on the kitchen floor with my wet feet from the shower, I switch on the TV. Silence unsettles me; I don't really know why, but I prefer noise to be going on around me all the time, it helps me concentrate.

After settling on some old detective show, I turn my attention to my outfit. Flinging open my wardrobe doors I let the contents spill out over the floor. I think I should probably tidy up later, but you never know, today could change everything so that I won't have to because I'll be able to afford a cleaner to do it for me, which would be handy because I'm pretty sure housework is the thing I am worst at in the world, other than Maths that is. Bending down I start to rummage through the shoes gathered at the bottom of the wardrobe, sending odd ones flying, along with garments of clothing which happen to be burying them. No, none of these scream 'look at me I should be famous', or 'look at my style, isn't it fantastic?', or even 'Ben, how hot do I look right now?' Wait a minute, what about my hidden shoebox! Sitting back, I drag the box out from beneath my bed and, taking the lid off, I hold back a gasp as I see, sitting on top, the beautiful (could have bought a car for the price of them) stilettos!

Perfect! God, I can't believe I nearly forgot about these! I really should have them out on display but the questions would be too much, plus everyone would want to steal them, and the last time I loaned a pair out they came back with a smudge across the toe of one them! Can you believe that? A smudge, a bloody great big black smudge across a pair of gorgeous patent red kitten heels and not even an apology with them, bloody cheek! Right, so I have the shoes sorted and I still have, how long, two hours, not bad – now for the rest of the outfit. Well it's going to have to be a longer pencil skirt now because of my stupid computer getting in the way. Oh I know, I could wear that silver-grey one I bought the other week, I've been looking for a place to wear it and what to wear with it. How about that white satin shirt? No that's impossible, it's in the dry cleaners after I spilt rosé wine down it last week. Plus I'll be on TV, which adds pounds anyway, so white really isn't a sensible way to go. Standing up I remove the towel from my head, which has 'de-turbaned' and is now just getting in the way, and begin sifting through the shirts that are still hanging on the rail. I really must invest in a new wardrobe – the volume of clothes I have seems to be making this one look like it's ready to collapse. Pulling out a black silky shirt, which has some frill-like detail to the front, I hold it up against the skirt. "Brilliant," I say aloud, that matches perfectly, and finished off with that diamond necklace with matching earrings I got from my dad the last time he went away on business I will look amazing!

I should be a personal shopper I think, I have a great eye for what suits people. And that scratch on my leg isn't even going to be noticeable, which is good; I just hope Dan looks as good as me, then we will be the best-looking writing duo ever to hit the world!

Damn – only an hour left before he picks me up… I really need to get ready now.

* * *

Two and a half hours later and my head is spinning. We drove here at about two hundred miles an hour, which may have been slightly my fault when I insisted on going back into my flat about six times to change handbags, bracelets and my hair, but still, he didn't need to drive that fast, did he? It's just a good job that after a whirlwind tour of the studios, which are massive and horrifically scary, I'm really glad I didn't have any breakfast because now I do feel a little sick. We are sat down in a make-up room and they begin touching up my make-up and fixing my hair for me, which is useful seeing as by now my hair resembles the hair I have the morning after a very messy night out – minus a few twigs from falling in bushes on the way home – and I have the whole sweating under the make-up thing going on, which has made my face look a little bit like it's melted.

The girl doing my hair is really nice and keeps asking me questions about why I am going to be on the TV, and by the time she is finished and I am being led to the set I have practised everything I want to say with her; she was very helpful. Dan is waiting for me by the camera where we have to walk on from. Oh wow, this is amazing and so scary! This could change everything for me, I could be famous after today. I stand looking around in awe, craning my neck to see as far up as I can. The cameras and lights – it's all incredible! Taking a step back my heels catch a lead and I try to regain my footing, but before I know it I have gone flying, and in grabbing out for something to steady me on the way down I grab the cameraman and manage to pull his trousers right down with me. So there I am, lying in an unceremonious heap on a pile of wires while the cameraman glares at me, wrestling to pull his trousers up. I look at Dan, waiting for him to help me up, but he is bent double from laughing. Fat lot of good he is being. So I struggle to my feet on my own and notice that I've only gone and laddered my bloody tights, bugger!

"You are a clumsy twat." Bloody cheek of him. I am not

clumsy, I just have impaired balance; it's all to do with my inner ear or something.

"I am not," I answer back sulkily.

"Did you have to pull his trousers down?"

"He should have worn a belt shouldn't he, that's hardly my fault," I reason quite convincingly, although I get the feeling he doesn't think so.

Ten minutes pass with me being sulkily silent towards him before we are ushered forward onto the sofas, where we are joined by Ben and his co-host Kate Garraway. God, Ben is even hotter in real life. I really should start going for the older man again, Dan and James are just too immature. Yeah, that's what it is, they are the ones to blame, not me, I need a man who will respect me and… oh bollocks, he just asked me a question and I have no idea what it was. I look to Dan while I stutter at him, and luckily he is on form today and rescues me.

Smiling as widely and professionally as I can, most of the interview goes without a hitch. I manage to say nearly everything that Marie told me to say, not that any of it's true. I bloody hate her, but in my best attempt at acting (I think that A-Level in drama has paid off) I chat away about how our wonderful Editor has given us free rein to follow our instincts. This is a complete load of rubbish, as she dictates everywhere we go and even cuts down my articles when I've written them! I wrote a great piece about the best shoes to take to Milan and she made me change the whole thing. Looking down briefly I catch sight of Kate's shoes.

"I have those in purple," I say before I can stop myself. I can feel Dan freeze beside me as Ben and Kate look around them, not knowing what the bloody hell I was talking about.

"I'm sorry?" stutters Kate.

"The shoes," I blush, realising that I have just made a complete fool out of myself on national TV. "Your shoes, I have the same ones in purple. Sorry, I have a bit of a shoe thing," I clarify when they still look slightly confused.

"Oh… well I guess you get to see all the best shoes around when you're travelling," says Ben, now sweating slightly.

Okay, so that's my relationship with him down the toilet now he thinks I'm a raving loon with a shoe fetish. I can't believe I can't even hold concentration on a TV show, I think I have a serious problem. I need a therapist.

"Yes, especially when we visit the cities. Paris and Milan are two places that are great for shoe shopping. I mean, that's what we do – Dan does the bloke things and writes about how good a place is for a man to visit, so he goes to see the football stadiums and stuff, and I go shopping. Then couples read the articles and decide whether it's the right place for them to go." I think that was a good enough recovery; I mean you never know, they might not even notice the whole accidental shoe comment.

"So, does it put a strain on your relationship to work together so closely all the time?" asks Kate, trying to steer the conversation in a new direction.

"Oh no, not really, we're still really close, aren't we?" I answer, automatically turning to Dan and beaming.

"Erm… yeah," he stutters, looking even more flustered than the rest of the crew.

"So it's true then, you are a couple?" Kate pipes up, as the audience lets out an 'ohh'.

Bollocks, I think I may have just inadvertently told the whole country that Dan and I are a couple.

"I... erm." What do I say?

"I'm sorry, that's all we have time for..." interrupts Ben, as the camera pans to him and he starts introducing the next segment. Shit!

Well, I never thought I'd hear myself say that I was glad being on TV was over, but I really am! I mean, I enjoyed most of it, but the falling over, laddering my tights, mentioning Kate's shoes out loud live on air and then not getting Ben's number or even a kiss afterwards kind of ruined it a little bit. But at least I didn't destroy the whole day and the relationship between the magazine and 'GMTV' is intact, and they've invited us to come back in a year to do a follow-up type show, which is good because at least I won't get fired. Well, not for this balls-up anyway.

The journey home is a little frosty to put it lightly. Dan seems to agree that we now look like a couple, which is totally their fault. I mean, they got me all confused, and he seems to be upset. I have to admit that I am very much uninhibited by this view... but there you go.

"I can't believe this," he fumes, "what is Chloe going to say?"

"Who cares?" I say before I can stop myself. Shit, this has got to be some sort of disease. I really need to see someone about it before I get shot or something.

"I do!" he snaps.

"Well she knows it's not true, so what difference does it make?"

"All the bloody difference. You don't get it, it's not like you've got a bloke sitting at home watching you look to the whole world like you're going out with me."

Alright, no need to go there, was there? Talk about rubbing it in.

"And to top it off you had to go and start talking about bloody shoes again, didn't you?"

Seriously, has the bloke got no tact? I don't think I like him much any more. You know, there is such a thing as going too far. Maybe I'll forgive him though – he does look beautiful in that shirt – but not for a while. He needs to learn a lesson. So when he drops me off I slam the door and storm off without even saying goodbye, which makes me feel really bad straight away, so I text him to say thanks for the lift.

Walking into my empty flat I take off my shoes and place them carefully in the hidden shoebox, where they will stay until I need to make a fool of myself in front of the next bloke. And after making a cup of tea, I turn to my room. Right, okay, so today wasn't the earth-shattering change I was expecting, and I don't think I will have a cleaner any time soon, so I guess I'd better start cleaning this myself.

Chapter Nine
Contemplation, planning, more shopping

It's quite funny when you think of it actually. I see the same people every single day on this train, that's when I catch the early one; so I see two sets of people, depending on which train I get on. That's like a hundred people or something, and I never talk to any of them, unless I'm telling them to get off my shoes. Although the ones I see all the time know not to stand anywhere near them now, so I don't even have to say that to them. Just think... I could have a long-lost cousin sitting next to me everyday and I would never know! The train pulls to a squeaky halt and I jump off quickly, regretting the decision immediately as I nearly topple over and twist my ankle, forcing me to limp the rest of the way into work.

"Morning, Sophie," a voice suddenly interrupts my thoughts. Am I in the office already? Bloody hell, I must have limped faster than I usually walk. Maybe it's because I didn't stop off for my usual muffin today – why didn't I? I spend the next few minutes travelling up in the lift pondering this very complex and confusing issue, until I suddenly remember that I had one before I left this morning and decided that it would be a little too fattening, even for me, to have two in one morning, especially as I have to lose about a stone if I'm ever going to fit into my dress for Ruth's wedding in January.

"Morning," I say brightly, smiling as I stroll through the noisy office towards my desk. I love this place when it's busy, it's so vibrant and full of all kinds of interesting people – some I see every time I'm in the office and others I don't recognise, probably doing freelance work or temping. Reaching my desk, I dump my bag next to my chair and sit down, moving a few pieces of paper around, okay a few piles of paper and stuff, until I can see my keyboard. Two hours later I have just finished proofreading my final draft of the Tuscany article and click 'send' – and it is off my hands and into the hands of the Sub-Editor. Good morning's work if I do say so myself.

Now, where did I put that planner? I'm sure there's something else I should be doing, it's niggling at the back of my mind. I disappear beneath a pile of rubbish on my desk and emerge, slightly red in the face but nevertheless triumphant, a few minutes later. Ah that was it, I have to write a short piece on London transport for tourists for next week's issue.

Time for lunch I think, as I reckon I've been working on that article for like three hours already and that's long enough!

I wander into TopShop (another one of my favourite lunchtime haunts) – it's so big and full of wonderful sales that I genuinely sometimes get lost, and have been told off for taking a slightly longer than contracted lunch hour. But that time was honestly not my fault, the woman just took forever bringing out my shoes and then the queue was just ridiculously long. I mean for God's sake, what were that many people doing in TopShop at one in the afternoon on a Tuesday?

Seeing as I now have to fit five floors into less than an hour, I flick quickly through the sale racks and pick up a little black vest top with diamantes around the neckline, and head for the shoes. Now those are beautiful, they really look like God himself could have made them. Granted, they are probably not to everybody's taste, but if you appreciate good shoes then you will definitely see the beauty in them. A five-inch heel complete with an inch wedge under the toes too, patent red leather, perfect for work, weddings, sex… if you're into all that, which I'm not – honestly! I'll leave that sort of stuff to people less clumsy, because I'm sure if I were to try it disasters would happen and ambulances would be involved.

The best thing about these shoes is that they have them in blue and black too, so I can get a new pair next week and the others the week after that. Brilliant, and I get to buy new outfits to match them. I'm pretty sure that my bank manager would have a fit if he saw my reasoning for spending, although it would clear up the reason for my overdraft for him.

"Sophie, is that you?" The shop assistant is peering at me from behind several boxes of shoes.

"Hello, Kerri, how are you?"

"I'm good, thank you, I haven't seen you in a while. Finally stopped buying shoes?"

"Not exactly," I grin, holding out the shoes that seemed to have magically appeared in my hands. When I picked them up, I had clung to them as if someone was going to rip them from my hands!

"You want these ones?" she laughs.

"Yes, please."

"Okay, I'll just get them for you, size…"

"Six," I say, tapping my fingers on my legs, wanting to hold them in my hands now.

"Here they are," she smiles, as she walks towards me holding out the box.

"Thanks," I say, "I'll just pay for them now." I stand by the till holding out my card to her at arm's length, trying not to shout at her to hurry up so I can stroll back to work with my new amazing shoes and wear them on the next night out.

Stepping out into the cold October wind, I pull my coat closer around me. I reach for my phone and excitedly dial Ruth's number and wait for her to answer.

"Ruth Jones speaking."

"Hey, babe."

"Oh hey, Soph, what's up?"

"Just out on lunch, guess what?" I say, my voice squeaky with excitement.

"Erm… you recently spent the evening with an amazing director who lives in Hollywood?"

"How did you guess?" I say, disappointed that my moment of thunder had been stolen. I hate it when that happens. This also means that now everybody will know the news before I tell them. Bloody Emily – such a gossip. I mean you would never catch me doing anything like that, not in a million years.

"You've blatantly been stalking me again, haven't you?" I say, trying to inject some sternness into my voice and failing miserably.

"What, moi?" she feigns surprise, giggling down the other end of the phone at me. "No, Emily phoned me this morning to talk about Friday night."

"Oh yeah, I forgot about that – where are we going?"

"Just a bar in town for a few drinks."

"I thought we were going up to London and making a big night of it?" Again I am disappointed, I was looking forward to that.

"Yeah we were, but Carly can't make it; she's not coming up for another week now."

"But…"

"I know, I spoke to her this morning though and she got caught up with work."

"The girl does my head in, I had everything planned," I exclaim.

"I know, but she did say to tell you that 'The Love' sends her love and that she is bringing you some of that homemade garlic lemon mayonnaise."

"Alright then, I'll forgive her," I smile.

"Good, so you still coming on Friday?"

"You know me, anywhere there's a drink and a Ruth I'm there," I say loudly, realising that half the street has now stopped to look at me.

"Okay cool, I will see you at half seven in Wetherspoons then and we'll go from there."

"I'll be with Emily, so you'd better make that half eight," I remark, as we say our goodbyes and I head back to the office to finish the afternoon.

* * *

It's half past four and I've nearly finished the first draft of that transport thing with my headphones on, when a voice behind nearly makes me have a heart attack.

"Sophie, can I have a word?" Bloody people sneaking up on me.

"Oh, yes of course," I reply almost nervously. I hate Marie. I mean I know she's my boss and everything, but she scares the shit out of me, and I don't think she really likes me either.

"Come into my office." She turns on her heel and I hurry behind her, trying to keep up.

"So," I say, not exactly sure why I had started talking as I had nothing to say. Bugger, quick, think of something to say.

"Anyway, this will have to be quick, I have a meeting in five minutes." Her voice is as stiff and stern as ever and I feel like a school child that has just been sent to see the head teacher. I do, however, try to remain professional and crease my brow in an attempt to look interested in what she is saying.

"I don't know whether you've heard the rumours, but I'm taking a month or two's leave as of next week."

Bloody hell it's true, she is pregnant, or is it that she is eloping? I personally like the one where she got the sack just for being a bitch, but I don't think that's true.

"So, I want to tell you where you are visiting and writing

about for the next couple of issues, as they've changed slightly."

Oh, I was really looking forward to going to Milan as well.

"January's issue you will be going to the Christmas markets in Düsseldorf," she is consulting her notebook as she continues, "and for the February's issue you will be going back to Paris, but I want an article geared only towards the sights and restaurants, a romantic getaway, getting ready for Valentine's Day, rather than on the shopping this time. For March's issue, I want a piece on Vienna."

Wow, okay, I can deal with not going to Milan. I scribble all this down and then look back at her waiting for her to finish what she was saying, but she seems distracted. Crap, what should I do, just stand here or back away quietly?

"Can you pass that information along to Dan for me, please?"

"Yeah, erm, I mean yes, sure."

"Okay well, I'll see you tomorrow then," she says, giving me my signal to leave.

Wow, this is like the biggest piece of gossip I've got my hands on in literally years, I can't wait to get home and tell Emily, and phone Dan. I sit at my desk fidgeting as I check my Facebook account and wait as the minutes tick by until I can leave, without looking like I'm skiving.

*   *   *

Well that was the longest journey home ever; the whole way I was just bursting to tell someone my gossip. I was even tempted to tell the man sitting next to me on the train, but I think he was more interested in his can of lager than me anyway. Reaching the door I fumble with the key in my hurry to get in, and bursting in call out to Emily, only to hear my own voice echoing back to me. Damn, she must be at Sam's. A quick check of the whiteboard confirms my suspicions:

> Soph, I'm staying at Sam's tonight, see you
> tomorrow.
> P.S. We have no milk left!
> Em xxx

I'll have to settle for just telling Dan then – it's never as much fun though, men just don't get the whole gossip thing. Flicking on the television I wander into the kitchen and have to settle for a black coffee and some cheese and crackers; really need to do some shopping tomorrow. Heading back to the living room, I find 'Hollyoaks' and grab the phone. As I am dialling his number – it's sad I know, but I have memorised it – I am once again bubbling with excitement at the thought of telling him my gossip.

"Dan Shorely." That's odd, his voice doesn't sound as sexy as usual. Maybe it's because I spent most of the other night talking to James.

"Hey, Dan, it's Sophie."

"Oh hi, Sophie, you alright?"

"Yeah I'm good, thanks. Where were you today?"

"Oh yeah, I was in the Birmingham office."

"What were you doing up there?"

"I was writing a piece on the north of England, and they said I could work there."

"Oh." Odd, why didn't he tell me? Well I suppose he isn't my boyfriend, yet. "Anyway," I continue, suddenly remembering why I had phoned him, "you'll never guess what I found out today."

"What?" He doesn't sound interested at all, bloody men.

"Marie's taking leave for the next month or two."

"You know that's just a rumour, right?"

Cheeky bastard.

"No. She called me into her office today and told me."

"Really?"

Ha, now he's interested.

"Yep, and she's changed our next three articles."

"What?"

"I know, but don't worry they're still good. So why do you think she's going away?"

"I don't know. Sophie, what do you mean she's changed the next three articles?"

"I mean we are going to Düsseldorf, Paris and Vienna instead."

"Bugger!"

Okay, little worried. Why is he not wondering why Marie is going away but is all cut up about Milan? He's been there like three times already.

"What's wrong?" I say, confused.

"Nothing, look, I'm going to have to go, sorry, Soph."

"But…"

"I'll see you tomorrow."

"But…"

"Bye." The line goes dead.

What the bloody hell was that all about? Now, instead of getting my gossip off my chest, I am left with even more – not only is Marie taking 'unexpected' leave, but Dan doesn't seem to care and he is upset about our trips changing for the better. My life is seriously turning into a soap opera right now. Maybe I could write myself into 'Hollyoaks', at least that way I could get myself a man. I could just write it in.

Chapter Ten
Here come the girls

Smashing my hand down on the alarm clock I yelp in pain and sit up, rubbing my sore fingers. Why the bloody hell did I set the alarm this early? It's Saturday, for God's sake. Flopping back down onto the pillows I grab the remote and flick on the TV. That's funny, what is 'This Morning' doing on on a Saturday, I mumble, as I flick over quickly and see 'GMTV'. What's going on here and why... oh shit, it's Friday isn't it, and I've overslept again. Bugger!

Jumping up quickly, I run to the shower, and after a record-breaking time of twenty-five minutes I am half-dressed and pretty much ready to go. However, thinking about it I realise that no one really ever notices when I'm late anyway, which is pretty much everyday, because the office is always so busy with people coming in and out. Also, Dan has got quite good at covering for me, which is a bonus and could be his secret way of showing his love. A girl can dream, can't she?

Adding the last touches to my make-up and resorting to a messy bun as my hair seems to be refusing to dry this morning, I head out of the door and get halfway down the stairs before I realise I have no skirt on over my tights! I run back as quickly as possible, waving at old Mrs Graham who is trying to tell me something but just looks too dumbfounded to do anything other than stay rooted to the spot, as she notices my lack of clothing. Re-emerging five minutes later, she is still standing there, opening and closing her mouth like a goldfish, so I trot past her and try to pretend nothing has happened,

"Morning, Mrs Graham." Okay, I think I may have got away with that one, just about.

Strolling into the office, a smile spreads across my face as I breathe in the familiar smell of hot paper from the printer and coffee. Oh, do you know what, I really fancy a doughnut right now. I wonder if I can persuade that work experience kid to go and get some from down the road. Picking up the phone, I dial Barry's internal number and wait for him to answer. I know it's a bit lazy, but he is all the way over at the other side of the office.

"Hey, Barry," I say cheerfully as he picks up the receiver.

"Sophie, why are you phoning me when I can practically hear you from here anyway?" he mocks. Honestly, he really can't hear me, I'm not that bloody loud.

"Because I would have got told off for shouting across to you."

"Right, okay then, I guess that makes sense." Ha, yet another point won by me.

"So what did you want anyway? You don't normally communicate with anyone until midday." Well that's blatantly a lie; honestly, anyone would think I don't like mornings or something.

"I was just wondering…"

"Yes?"

"… if maybe what's-his-name, you know, little work experience person, could maybe go get some doughnuts for everyone," I hold my breath as I wait for his reply.

"For everyone?" he repeats in a questioning tone.

"Yes," I say. Well, I couldn't exactly get him to go and get them just for me, could I? I guess I'll just have to put it on my credit card, maybe I could claim it back as work expenses or something.

Half an hour later, I have munched my way through two big jam doughnuts and am contentedly sipping on my black coffee. I think today's going to be a good day, as long as I get this research finished. Oh God, and I've got to get the Tuscany article sent over too, which, as I glance over it, I have to admit is bloody fantastic. God I'm good, no wonder they love me here. Tapping away, I hum along to the radio and don't notice the time flying by until my phone rings, and glancing at the little display on my screen see that it is nearly one o'clock. Picking up the phone I put on my most professional voice as I wait to hear who is on the other end.

"Soph, hi, it's Becca."

"Oh hey, babe, what you up to?" This is a nice surprise, I haven't spoken to her in ages.

"Oh nothing much, I was just wondering what the plan was

for tonight?"

"Tonight?" What is she talking about? I don't remember making any plans for tonight, and I'm pretty sure I haven't been drunk for ages, well at least not for a couple of weeks, and I never plan that far in advance. "Erm…" Okay stall her, good plan, maybe she will just tell me without me having to ask.

"Yeah, girls night out, remember?"

Oh God, is that tonight? That whole waking up and thinking it was Saturday really threw me off arrangements today. Oh that means I'll have to take my lunch to go get a new outfit then. Good job I ate those doughnuts this morning so I won't be too hungry; maybe my brain was planning in advance for me, or would that be my stomach?

"Sophie, you still there?"

Must remember not to daydream whilst having a phone conversation.

"Oh right, yeah, erm, well do you want to get a cab into town with me and Em from our place then?"

"Yeah, sounds good to me," she replies cheerfully.

"Cool, okay then, get round mine for about seven then," I say.

"Right okay, I'll see you then. Have to go, break-time is over and I have a classroom of delinquents to get back to."

I laugh, knowing full well that she loves her job, even if the kids are mental and half of them should, or probably do, have ASBOs.

"Alright babe, see you then." Hanging up the phone I smile to myself as the familiar excitement of an impending messy night out starts building in the pit of my stomach. So, lunchtime panic, outfit shopping, which I have found I am a natural at, and that has absolutely nothing to do with the fact that I have a knack for forgetting I have arranged to go out until the last minute.

*   *   *

Getting home I run through to my room, dumping my bags on the bed. I managed to find a gorgeous little cream and gold dress that I plan to wear with black leggings and these beautiful gold, strap-up sandal stilettos. They have a black wooden base and heel, which is about four inches, and thick gold straps, almost like those gladiator sandals that are in fashion at the moment. I love them, and the best bit is that they only cost thirty-five quid. Stripping off quickly, I wrap my towel around me and head for the shower. I can hear Emily singing in her room and can tell from the state of the bathroom that she has already showered. Blimey, am I later than I thought, or has she actually, finally, almost got the hang of getting ready on time?

I was wrong, she hasn't, it is twenty past eight and Becca and I have been sitting in the living room drinking wine and waiting for her since ten past seven. We are now on our second bottle, feeling quite tipsy already, and the taxi will be here in about five minutes. But Emily has decided that she wants to change again because her shoes completely clash with her top, although that may be slightly my fault.

"Em, the taxi's here," I yell, as my phone rings for a couple of seconds and I jump up, narrowly avoiding spilling my wine all over Becca as I grab my bag.

"Okay, I'm ready," comes the reply as we all converge at the door, and after a quick double check of ID, money and keys, we head down to the cab and to town.

Walking into the overcrowded pub, we fight our way to the bar and buy our drinks before pushing through the people to find Ruth, Tanya and Kate sitting at a table at the back, chatting animatedly about something.

"Hey," I call as I reach them, and the usual hellos, hugs and kisses are exchanged before we fight over getting chairs, and eventually manage to obtain two stools, which Becca and I sit on as Emily perches on the edge of Kate's chair.

"Sorry we're late," I say, glancing at Emily and giggling before changing the subject. "So, where are we off to tonight then?" I ask, looking expectantly from one face to the next.

"Oh, I don't know, I just thought we'd wing it a bit, see where the hotties seem to be heading and follow them," says Ruth, with a cheeky glint in her eye.

"Hey, you're a taken woman, but I do like your thinking."

"Well there's no harm in looking, is there? I mean, with some of the talent that appears to be out tonight, I'm pretty sure it would be a crime not to look."

We all laugh, and talk continuously like this for the next hour or so, until it is time for us to move on and find a club.

Standing up, I'm not the only one who wobbles, and as we head out into the cold wind and head towards the club we had finally decided on, it is slow going, partly because of the random pausing to try and remain upright, and partly because I suddenly have an overwhelming urge to stop and talk to a couple of policemen, who even let me have my photo taken with them. Mind you, that may be because Emily told them that I was leaving the country for the next two years after tonight to do missionary work in Africa!

*   *   *

Four hours later and I'm exhausted – I danced up until the point when I fell over and bruised my arse, and my ego. And, as I stumble out into the cold, I head straight towards the smell of cheesy chips. By the time I get into the cab my shoes are in my hand, and I am vaguely aware that I seem to have lost the other girls and that for some reason there is a bloke sitting next to me. Hmm, okay so I have no idea who this man is, but he seems to know me and is chatting away while I smile at him, hoping he would disappear or something, but he seems to be staying put. Oh well, I'll tackle this one later. The cab suddenly comes to a stop and before I know it I am standing outside, watching it drive away with the random man still inside… luckily. Well that was weird, but right now I am really tired and I think I'm quite drunk too, so maybe bed is the best place. So crawling up the outside stairs I find the door and after about ten minutes manage to get inside.

*   *   *

Waking up I feel as though my head is on fire, and my eyes are glued together with mascara and eyeliner. Rolling over onto my back I flinch suddenly; ouch, my arse really hurts, what did I do last night? Oh yeah that's right, I fell. A sudden flashback of me lying in a heap in the middle of the dance floor makes me cringe. Sitting up and rubbing my eyes until they open, I realise that not only am I still fully dressed apart from my shoes, which are on my pillow for some reason, but my door is wide open and the contents of my purse, including my phone, are strewn across the hallway. Getting up very slowly, to avoid being sick, I walk, hunched over, to the kitchen, fearing that if I stand up straight I may die of brain explosion or something.

"What happened to you last night?" says Emily from the sofa, making me jump.

"Jesus, Em, you scared me," I scream, instantly regretting all the movement and shouting as my stomach lurches, and I sit down quickly to avoid being sick all over the living room floor.

"Sorry, sweetheart, you look like shit by the way."

"Thanks," I say sarcastically. "What happened to you lot anyway?"

"I can't really remember," she laughs. "We all decided to leave when Tanya started throwing up in the toilets, and we thought you were with us, but by the time we got to the cab you were gone."

"Well I have no idea. I ended up in a cab with some random bloke, and then I was here this morning," I snigger, as I try and piece the night together.

"You're a nightmare, woman, you know that?" she smiles, as the theme tune for 'Will and Grace' starts playing in the background, and so making myself a coffee, I settle down onto the sofa and into my usual Saturday routine.

Chapter Eleven
Ruined chances... again!

I can't believe it's December already. My little brother is officially married and I haven't bought a single present either, and in a couple of weeks I'll have to spend yet another Christmas without a bloke. Oh and I've just thought, my brother's going to have his bloody wife there. The wedding was incredible though, it was like a fairytale. I can't believe it was nearly two weeks ago – I think I am still suffering the effects of the champagne. The whole thing was completely, well, completely posh really. But it was amazing, and must have cost her parents so much, but it was all done very nicely. Although to be honest, I think if I had been given more of a role in the day, it may have been just a touch... well, a touch more stylish!

Well there's not much hope of solving the problem of Christmas without a man, but at least I can pick up all my presents while I'm in Germany so I don't need to think about that for now, and I might be lucky and catch a sale or two, which reminds me, I have to ask Dan whether he can pack lightly as I have a feeling I may exceed the weight limit on the way back.

Sometimes, I feel like I'm almost living out of a suitcase. Not that I mind, I mean I get paid to travel the world and write – there is no better job, not for now anyway. But my room is a total tip at the moment and I should tidy it, but I think I'll wait until I get back before I do that. Right in the middle of the floor stands my brand new suitcase – it's a beautiful bright red, from Harrods! I know, I know, but I kind of got forced into buying it. You see, I go in there now and again, okay almost every lunchtime, just to look around at all the beautiful things I can't afford but think about buying when I win the lottery or something. So anyway, I was in there one day last week looking at the suitcases and a couple were in there too, and I saw the shop assistant asking them to leave because they were saying how it was too expensive and they weren't going to buy anything. I couldn't bear to get thrown out of my favourite lunchtime haunt, so I just grabbed the suitcase – I mean I needed a new one anyway – and bought it. Only problem is that it is quite big, nearly as big as me, so I have no idea where I'm going to put it. Plus, when I told Emily she wasn't impressed.

'How can someone who has eight suitcases already possibly need a new one?' was all she had said. I did try and explain to her that two of them were on the way out anyway so I was going to throw them, and I do have to travel a lot. It's like her needing new, I don't know, brushes or a dust remover, or bone finder thingies! But she didn't seem that impressed. I guess she can only see the fact that our little flat was becoming full of suitcases. Oh well, I offered to pay for the pizza tonight to make up for it, so she's happy enough, for now. My only problem is that if she reacted like that to the suitcase, I just hope to God she doesn't find my secret shoe stash any time soon.

The only bad thing about this Christmas trip is that we are being sent to catch the full Christmas atmosphere, which means that we aren't coming back until Christmas Eve, late in the evening too. I think my mum nearly cried when I told her. We're quite up with our traditions in our family and I think this will be the first year I can ever remember that I won't be singing round the Christmas tree on Christmas Eve, and the first time I can ever remember not waking up in my bed at home on Christmas morning. Oh my God, I'm not going to have a stocking! My eyes suddenly fill with tears as I realise that the tradition of a lifetime will be broken for the first time. Now I understand how my mum felt, and the tears are rolling down my cheeks as I think about the fact that I won't be able to spend the time I want to with my family.

Oh wow, okay, so whilst I feel slightly better about the whole situation I think drinking half a bottle of vodka and scoffing an entire tub of Ben and Jerry's last night may have been going over the top, as I now feel slightly sick. To top it off, I leave for Germany in the morning and Dan hasn't even spoken to me yet, so I have no idea of any of the plans because he takes care of all of that (since the Rome fiasco) and now I have to get up and pack. At least I can avoid going into the office today. Marie's not there any more as she started her leave a few weeks ago, and packing for my trip is much more important than dragging my very hung-over self into a crowded office.

Instead, I drag myself into the kitchen for some coffee and a glass of water, and heading back to my room I open the curtains and pull my Harrods suitcase up onto my bed to start the long process of deciding what to pack. A lot of people underestimate the importance of packing; I mean, it can be crucial to the success of a trip, so I always take extra care to make sure I have packed for every possible eventuality.

I'm just finishing the third repack of my case when my phone begins to blare out Justin Timberlake's 'Lovestoned'; one day I will learn that changing my ringtone everyday is not a helpful thing. Reaching for it, I look at the display and flip it open.

"Hey, Dan."

"Sophie, you free for me to pop round?"

"Err yeah, I suppose so, can you give me an hour?"

"Yeah that's fine, just need to talk over the plans for tomorrow with you."

"Oh okay, well I'll see you in an hour then."

"Cheers, Soph, bye."

As the phone line goes dead I keep mine to my ear for a second. Weird, why does he want to come over to talk about something he would usually say on the phone? Catching sight of myself in the mirror I nearly scream. Shit, I look like… well I look like shit! And he's going to be here in an hour! Dropping everything I run to the bathroom. Now only fifteen minutes before he gets here and looking at myself in the mirror I have to say I'm impressed with myself. I suppose that's why I'm a writer, the way I thrive under pressure. Of course there's slightly less pressure if you're organised, but I'm not, so I have to deal with the pressure bit.

I'm sitting on my sofa staring at Dan and I can feel my face flushing with anger. How dare the bloody bastard look like he's sorry or nervous?

"Listen, Sophie, it's just that Chloe has to go away over Christmas so she wants to spend some time with me." He's acting like he's just cheated on me or something.

"But I thought in Tuscany you were saying…"

"I know, but I was wrong, I think it was just the wine talking."

Tell me he didn't just say that. I knew it – we had a moment, it wasn't just in my imagination and now he was feeling guilty. I am not going to let him get away with this.

"We hadn't had any wine." Okay so that may be a lie and we might possibly have had a good couple of bottles, but I am not letting him get away with that excuse.

"Look, Sophie, we're mates, right?"

Did he honestly just use the mates line?

"Yes, but what does that have to do with anything?"

"It's just that, well, me and Chloe, we were going through a rough patch and, well you were so good at listening…"

That's the first time anyone's ever said I'm good at listening.

"Dan, what's really wrong? I mean, why are you acting like we've slept together or something, we didn't even kiss?"

"Yeah, I guess we didn't, I've just been confused lately and I didn't want to upset you with the whole bringing Chloe to Germany thing."

When he says confused, does that mean he likes me? Bloody hell, I think Dan just said he liked me! Those shoes were magic,

I'm seriously going to wear them everywhere; or maybe it's that new face peel I bought.

"Sophie…" Oh shit he's still talking.

"Yes?" I say, trying to act like I'd heard what he had just said. Why is he looking relived?

"So you're okay with it then, I'll see you on Saturday?"

Bugger, I shouldn't have said yes and now I have to let him get away with it. I give a heavy sigh as I let him win, not that I know exactly what he is winning.

"Yes I'm okay, and yes, I will see you on Saturday."

"Thanks, Soph, I knew you'd understand." Getting up he gives me a kiss on the top of the head before leaving me in stunned silence. Wait until Emily hears about this one.

Chapter Twelve
Christmas Markets

My spirits are lifted as I reach the hotel. It's beautiful and not over the top posh either, although I bet the one Chloe and Dan are staying at is probably ridiculously expensive and makes this one look like a Travelodge.

No! Stop it, Sophie, I have a whole day to myself before I have to see her again and I will not think about her, I'm just going to enjoy myself. Pulling on my big fluffy boots I observe myself in the mirror: dark jeans, big boots and about four layers of tops and jumpers. I head out and find myself at the Altstadt (Old Town) in no time. The markets are all pretty quiet in the morning I heard and I must remember to put that in the article. But now, when it's just beginning to get dark, the place is packed solid, and there are market stalls everywhere, covered in lights, and moving Christmas Santas and Reindeer. Every other stall appears to be a food or drink stall and the smell of mulled wine and hot nuts is amazing. Oh and there are these potato Rosti things, which are served with apple sauce or garlic sauce, and they are the most amazing things I have ever tasted. Granted, I think I will need to go to the gym eight times a week for a year once I get back, but bloody hell they taste good.

The knick-knack stalls sell the most amazing little hand-carved wooden nativity pieces, candles and incense; well they sell everything really. After about two hours my hands are full of shopping bags. I've also popped into Kaufhof, which I've discovered is a bit like Debenhams, and found tons of bargains in there. This place is bloody amazing, I've only been here two hours and I've bought all my Christmas presents plus a few spares, three different Christmas Day outfits – so I can change after lunch and before high tea – and to top it off, I have discovered the most amazing potato food ever. Fuck Dan! I haven't even thought about him since I left the hotel. This, I have decided, is going to be my new tradition. I'm almost sad when I have to go back to the hotel and write my notes, but I am starting to feel a little sick… maybe I shouldn't have eaten so much, but I mean who can blame me? It's all there and so cheap, at least I think it's cheap. I haven't really got to grips with the whole euro thing yet, despite the number of places I visit where they use it.

The next morning, when I meet up with Dan and Chloe, we head out to a different part of the city and a different Christmas market. What I heard about the markets in the morning seems to be true. The place is empty and there are no stalls open yet, however all the other shops are and there's a Tchibo! I run in quickly to grab some coffee and emerge with a couple more presents for my dad and some extra coffee for Emily. By mid-morning the place has livened up a bit and my coffee stuff has been joined by a couple of tops and the most beautiful pair of shoes I saw in the window of a shop for only thirty euros. Chloe is staring at me like I'm crazy and I'm thinking the exact same thing about her – the woman's rich, I know that, and yet she hasn't bought anything. She has to be unbalanced – I should probably warn Dan. I'm getting quite hungry now because I haven't eaten anything and I get the feeling Chloe isn't the sort of person to eat anything ever, but by some miracle we do stop at a pub for lunch.

Note to self: remember for article, smoking ban definitely not in effect here, I feel like a smoke machine has just exploded in my face. But the soup we had – I think it was pea and sausage – was the best soup I've ever eaten, ever.

Okay, this is so much worse than Rome. I know that was one of the most romantic cities and everything, but here we are, it's Christmas and I'm a third wheel, but worse than that I'm in love with Dan, and since he told me that he is confused there has been this little flicker of light at the end of the tunnel.

But for now I have to watch the two of them all over each other, it's enough to make me throw up my lovely soup I just ate. I think the worst thing of all is that she's so bloody annoying, and weird. I mean what rich young woman, especially when they look like her, doesn't like to shop? It's just not normal.

"So," I say, not really because I have anything to say but more just to remind them that I'm still here, and that if they get any friskier with each other I'm going to feel like I should be paying to watch them! "Dan said you were going away for Christmas,

113

anywhere nice?"

"Oh not really, my parents don't like the cold so we always spend it at the villa in the Canaries."

'Not really'? The woman's mental! I notice Dan raising his eyebrows at me so I quickly shut my mouth.

"That sounds lovely," I say, trying to sound as if I have friends who regularly pop over to the Canaries. I think I pulled it off.

"What are you going to do over Christmas, Sophie?" she asks.

"Oh I'll spend it with my whole family like I do every year. Plus my brother's wife will be there too this year, they'll all come over…" I trail off, as I realise that she's not listening at all but is nibbling on Dan's ear. I flush slightly as I stare at him and he doesn't even look awkward – bastard. Oh I've had enough of this for one day, I'm leaving.

"Anyway, I've got some notes to write up, and a few more presents to pick up, so I'll see you two tomorrow, okay?" I stand up as I'm saying this and hand Dan some money to pay for my food.

"Oh okay, see you tomorrow." He didn't even look up! God, I am so over him! Okay, well not completely over him, but just give me until after Christmas and then I will be, definitely… well almost definitely.

Chapter Thirteen
Christmas with the family plus one

Christmas morning, I can't believe it. Turning over, I look at my clock and see that the display says eight a.m. Shit, I had better get up and get ready. My mum used the spare key to get in while I was away and when I got home last night there was my stocking sitting at the end of my bed. It isn't quite the same opening them on my own, so I called home and sort of was at home in a way after all, which cheered me up a lot.

An hour later, I glance in the mirror one last time. I have on my morning dress, a very formal black knee-length number, with just a hint of glamour in the sequined pattern across the neckline, and my secret black satin stilettos with the silver heels. I gather up two other outfits to change into and my stuff for tomorrow, and all the presents, which takes about three trips down to my car which is now looking quite overloaded.

Pulling up onto my parents' drive, I see that it is already full of cars belonging to everyone in my family and one very pretty black BMW that I don't recognise. Slotting myself neatly – well okay, after ten minutes of trying, I slot myself neatly – into a space and turn off the engine. Taking a deep breath to calm my excitement, I open the car door and, stepping out into the drizzle, I call out to my parents to come and help me as I try to pull the first bag off the back seat without sending everything else flying.

"Oh my baby, you're here at last! Come and give me a hug."

"Hi, Mum." Good God that woman can squeeze tight, I can't breathe. I'm actually seriously going to be the first person to die from hug crush injuries.

"Let's get inside before it starts raining again." It must have escaped her attention that it already is raining; I think maybe she's made a start on the mulled wine a little early.

"Oh hi, Dad, can you help me unload everything?" I give him a hug as he comes out in his slippers.

"I'm in the middle of making the starters at the moment, but I'll get Harry to come and help you. HARRY!" As he calls out, my brother comes striding out of the house wearing… is that an Armani suit? Bloody hell! I'll have to congratulate his missus later; she has obviously taught him style, something I've been trying to do for years.

I think maybe I'll cut down on presents next year; this is going to take forever to get them inside.

"Can I help?"

I freeze suddenly on the spot. I would know that voice anywhere, the only voice sexier than Vin Diesel's. Turning around slowly I meet the bright-green eyes that belong with the voice.

"What are you doing here?" I blurt out before I can stop myself.

He smiles back at me and, again, my knees nearly give way.

"Your brother invited me."

"James is on his own for Christmas. He can't fly over to his family because of work commitments, so I told him to come here," chips in Harry suddenly.

"I thought your family lived in Kent?" I ask confused.

"Oh they do but they flew over to Washington for a few months to visit my sister and I was supposed to be joining them, unfortunately though my filming schedule has been moved up, which means I can't get back over there," he replies.

"Oh, okay then, welcome to the family then, I guess." Did I just say welcome to the family? You're not bloody marrying him, Sophie! Honestly, I could shoot myself sometimes, and now I can feel my cheeks flaming. Change the subject, quick.

"Oh, you can take in this bag of presents," I say to James.

"At your service."

"Careful, it's heavy," I say, just as I see his muscles tense when he lifts it. Okay, so maybe I gave him the heavy bag on purpose, but if you go around wearing a tight shirt like that you're just asking for it. Now that I come to think of it I'm a genius, I mean anyone else would have taken the minimum, but prepared as always I have brought extras, so I can still give James a present. But only if he gives me one otherwise I'll just look stupid.

As I step into the house the smell of homemade bread rolls and mulled wine fills my nostrils. I love coming home to my dad's cooking. Much as I love living with Emily, and I do, takeaway pizza and Pot Noodles can get a bit samey. I step into the living room, and after greeting various family members for about twenty minutes I finally manage to grab a glass of warm Winter Pimms, which my dad has prepared especially for me, and some finger food, and slouch into the same old leather sofas that have sat in my living room since before I was born. I've found that as the years go by everybody seems to have grown out of the excitement of opening presents, except for my mum and me of course. So the present opening doesn't last that long and we all sit around talking and laughing, as my dad runs around like a mad man in the kitchen getting everything ready.

* * *

For the last three hours I have sat next to, opened my presents with and shared nearly all my Christmas secrets with a man I hardly know. A beautiful, well-dressed man who, incredibly, doesn't seem to be fazed by my family, not even my nan and mum together. It's very strange, and he's seemed so interested in everything I have to say. I can't wait to tell Emily all about this when she gets back from Sam's on Thursday. He even said I looked beautiful when I changed into my dinner outfit: a bronze strapless dress, with embroidered black flowers going up one side, and bronze stacked heels. He didn't say anything about my third outfit, but then that was just a new Pineapple tracksuit with a pink T-shirt from Mango, although I did have a really pretty pair of pink sandal-style stilettos to go with it, even if I did take them off as soon as I sat down. But right now, as I sit on the sofa next to him, eating my dad's homemade rolls stuffed with ham and leftover turkey, I'm really beginning to like this bloke. I mean, Dan has never even come in for a cup of tea with my parents.

I know he's supposed to be a bit of a bastard, and he does seem to be a bit snobby, but I'm sure everything Dan said about him couldn't be true. I mean he can't be that bad, can he? But what do I do about Dan? I've only just started to make a real breakthrough with him. He was so close to, you know, getting close to me in Tuscany and I think he might feel something. I have to keep going with my plans otherwise I'll just regret it forever. Then again, James is so hot and he seems to be quite into me, even if he does live on practically the other side of the world, and he could have a girlfriend waiting for him back there. Oh what to do, what to do? I think the best thing to do is to have some more of my dad's homemade potato salad and coleslaw, and give it some more thought. Maybe I could juggle both of them for a while? No. Bad idea. It will only end like that whole thing with Chris and Stuart – that was a complete disaster. I've drifted off again and now James has asked me something and I didn't hear a word, bollocks!

Oh God, this is the bit where we say goodnight. Okay, calm down, I can do this. It's not like today has been a disaster, is it? Okay, so Mum said he could stay the night because of the weather; a pretty thinly veiled excuse for keeping him here if you ask me, but he fell for it. Everyone else has gone to bed, while James and I stayed up to watch an old re-run of the 1984 version of 'A Christmas Carol', the one with George C Scott playing Scrooge, a film we, apparently, both love to watch, although I, personally, prefer the Muppets version but I'm not going to tell him that. Yawning, I stand up and, stretching my arms, decide to end the night before anything happens that I might regret.

"It's getting late," I say matter-of-factly.

"Yes, I suppose it is."

"I think I might head up to bed. Boxing Day tends to start pretty early around here," I say, pausing as I wait for his answer.

"That sounds like a good idea, it's been a tiring day." His voice is making my legs shaky.

"Oh I'm sorry, do you want me to show you where you'll be sleeping?"

"Yes thanks, that might help." I think there was a hint of sarcasm there but I'll let it pass for now.

We walk up the stairs slowly and creep along the corridor so as not to wake everybody up, and we come to a stop outside the door of the spare room. Turning to look at him I am aware of my breath rattling in my lungs a little, my body inches from his.

"So, goodnight," I whisper, in what I hope is my sexiest voice, and I gaze up at him waiting for him to kiss me passionately. I was already picturing us walking down the aisle, and then suddenly he was leaning closer. This was it, this was the beginning.

"Goodnight, Sophie," he whispers, stroking my hair out of my face and keeping his hand placed gently on my cheek, leaning closer towards me before grabbing my hand and sort of shaking it, and then promptly turns and walks into the room, closing the door in my face.

What the fuck! Did I just miss something or did he just completely play me? Dan was right, he is a complete bastard. I stomp into my room, not bothering to be careful about making noise, and sit up angrily in bed for a while weighing up the two men, until I finally decide that Dan was definitely still the way forward.

Chapter Fourteen
Dates coincide with jealousy

How the bloody hell did Dan find out about my disastrous Christmas with James? Well, not completely disastrous. I mean he was charming and brilliant with my family and we did get on really well, I just don't understand why he didn't kiss me. I thought I was finally over it, the whole men thing, after explaining everything to Emily over a meal of leftovers I had nicked from home. We had talked everything out and I had realised that he was just another idiotic man. But now I was going to get mocked by Dan, too. Bloody fantastic! Just when work was going well because Marie was gone, now I was going to have James thrown back in my face everyday. Still, I have to face him sooner or later and I haven't seen him in at least a week, so when I do I'll just forget all about James and why I ever thought I liked him in the first place. After showering and trailing a puddle of water into the kitchen, and multi-tasking as I got up a bit late this morning, I pour myself a bowl of Special K – part of my after-Christmas dieting regime.

Heading back into my bedroom, I flick on some music to wake myself up and, rolling my hair up turban-style in a towel, I wander to the wardrobe to pick out my outfit. After much deliberation, I decide on a grey and pink pinstripe pencil skirt suit, with a pale pink blouse, which I bought when we were in Rome. Oh and that pair of beautiful pink Dolce and Gabbana stilettos, with the little diamanté straps. I blow-dry my hair a bit and twist it up into a bun with little tendrils falling around my face, which I curl lightly with my straighteners. I then have a little singalong to the Leona Lewis 'Keep Bleeding' song, and hear Emily stirring in the next room. Oops, oh well it was time she was getting up now anyway. It takes me about ten minutes to finish doing my make-up, but as I stand up, grab my handbag and my coat and glance at myself in the mirror, I have to admit I look pretty good this morning. I might even stretch so far as to say damn hot, but that might just be the tiredness talking.

I get halfway down to my car before I realise that my handbag doesn't match my outfit and have to run back upstairs to pick out the pale pink Gucci one I bought a few months ago. Okay, so I may be twenty minutes late for the train, but perfection takes time and what I have going on this morning may even be enough to knock Dan off his feet. Or at least make him reconsider, plant an extra seed. I know he's been thinking about me since he found out about James spending Christmas with me. Note to self: must find out who told him. He has texted me at least ten times trying to find out what happened, all the details – the bloke's relentless.

I can see why he was such a good newspaper journalist before he started working with me. He simply doesn't give up until he has every single little piece of information he wants; that is when it concerns him or something he's vaguely interested in anyway, otherwise he just moans at me for gossiping and doesn't want to hear it. Hypocritical, that's what I call it!

* * *

Sitting on the train, I find my mind drifting back to my schooldays. I will never be able to get used to the whole going back to work between Christmas and New Year, it's really very disruptive. I mean usually, I have time to hit the sales, exchange some of my presents and find the most fabulous shoes to wear on New Year's Eve, and then later, an outfit to go with those shoes. Plus I don't see why I have to come into work. I mean, I know the whole getting paid thing helps, but the train is practically empty. Wait a minute, it's not Sunday is it? No of course not, everyone's just on holiday or having a good time, sleeping at seven in the morning. Well at least I look good – better when I don't look at the bags under my eyes too closely, but still pretty good. There's an old man, okay a middle-aged man, sitting opposite me reading a paper and I can't help but notice the grey bits in his hair. Come on, a little pride in your appearance please, all he has to do is buy some of that man hair dye that's on the TV and he'd easily look five years younger. I should be a presenter on 'Ten Years Younger' or something, you know. Thinking about it, it's always the hair that makes the biggest difference, that and the teeth. I do marvel at the number of people with disgusting teeth. Just go to a dentist already, brush them or floss regularly, anything to avoid wandering around with only two black stumps in your mouth. I remember this time once, when I was in university and was working in a shop part-time, this bloke used to come in and he had literally one tooth left. He used to breathe all over me and try to flirt, and it was all I could do not to throw up. It's a good job I'm a fantastic actress.

The train squeaks to a halt and I'm still staring intensely at the man opposite when he gets up and hops off, and I settle back into the seat, glancing out the window. Shit, this is my stop! I jump up and make a run for the door as it starts to close. Throwing myself off the train, I hit the wall, fall backwards and ladder my tights. Fuck that hurt, and bollocks, my tights are ruined. Okay, it's fine, I just need to get to work without anything else happening. Emerging out onto the street, I begin the ten-minute walk to the office and thankfully, it's not raining, so at least my make-up won't disappear before I get there. I start humming along to Jimmy Eat World's 'Hear You Me' before realising it was my phone ringing. Note to self: remember my previous notes to not change my ringtone everyday. Hastily, I grab for the slim hot-pink mobile and flipping it open put it to my ear.

"Hello, Sophie?" Oh God, why is he phoning me? He sounds so sexy, it's not fair.

"Hi, James," I stutter, stopping in the middle of the path as I try to calm myself down.

"I got your number off your brother."

"Oh right, cool." Did I actually just say cool? I might as well have snorted down the phone at him. I am such a tit.

"Yes. I was just wondering what you were doing this weekend?"

"This weekend, oh that's New Year's. I, er, I was just going to the office party." I can feel my face flushing as I try to control my shaky legs.

"I, well, I just found out that I can't get back to LA until the New Year."

Why does he sound as nervous as I feel? I don't understand.

"Oh that's a shame, I mean I bet you wanted to be home for New Year's Eve."

"Yes."

What do I say, what the bloody hell am I supposed to say?

"So what were you planning on doing then?" Okay, well that was supposed to be provocative, but probably just sounded like I have a really bad cold.

"Well, I was kind of hoping I could tag along to your party with you?"

I think he just asked me on a date, an actual date.

"What, like a date?" I splutter. Way to go, Sophie, make yourself sound like a complete and utter idiot, why don't you?

"Yes, unless you already have someone to go with?"

"Yes, I mean no, I don't have anyone to go with, I'd love to go with you." I finish speaking and nearly gasp for breath. Seriously, I think that maybe my heart is going to burst through my chest.

"Brilliant, so shall I pick you up on Saturday night then?"

"Yeah, that would be great thanks, erm bye."

"Sophie?"

"Yes?"

"I need your address."

"Oh, of course, sorry." I may have just turned redder than an actual tomato. "It's Flat 2 in the Lyndhurst Building, Stall Street."

"Okay great, I should be able to find it, I'll see you Saturday then."

"See you Saturday then. Bye."

"Bye." As the phone line goes dead I am still standing motionless on the spot. I can't quite believe what just happened, I mean this has really messed up my plans with Dan. Then again, a gorgeous movie director who lives in Hollywood has just asked me out. Me! This is the stuff they write films about. I feel like I'm actually in a happy version of the Truman Show or something and the people in charge are providing me with the perfect happy-ending scenario. Coming to my senses suddenly, I become aware of a man selling the Big Issue, staring at me in a very odd way, and also realise that I am, by now, very late for work.

*   *   *

By the time I get into the office I'm practically skipping, and as I trip over into the lift I realise why I haven't skipped since I started wearing heels. Oops, oh well, I have a date with someone from Hollywood and I get to rub it in Dan's face. That definitely beats posh Chloe and her private plane and boat. I bet James has met Orlando Bloom and Johnny Depp. Walking into the office, I decide to walk straight past Dan to my desk, being careful to show him my good side as I do so.

Sitting down, I switch on my computer and flick it to Facebook to check my messages. Bloody hell, not a single person has written on my wall since last night. Maybe I'll leave it a couple of hours and then casually add to my status that I have a hot date for Saturday, that will get everyone writing to me. I sit waiting for Dan to come over and talk to me but he doesn't, which is kind of annoying, although he does keep looking over at me. I can feel my legs twitching to run over and tell him, but I won't give him the satisfaction of me going to him. Okay, so I've waited ten minutes and I do have to go and photocopy some stuff, which means I have to walk past Dan's desk, and anyway, it would be rude to not say hello to him now, wouldn't it? I mean I haven't even asked him how his Christmas was. Right, that's it, I have to go over and say hello. Getting up, careful to walk over with my ruined tights facing away from him, I strut over slowly but purposely and stand by his desk, leaning on a pile of papers as I wait for him to look up.

"All right then, cheers mate, yeah, speak to you soon. Bye." Hanging up his phone, he leans back in his chair and gives me the cheeky smile that has been making my legs wobbly for the last three years.

"Hey," I say in my most business-like and sexy-office-lady way, I think.

"Hi, Soph, good Christmas?" He has that twinkle in his eye.

I can't believe him, he is just expecting it to have all gone horribly with James. Well I'll show him, won't I, bloody horrible, sexy, fantastic-smelling man.

"Actually, it was amazing," I say rather too snootily. "I just spoke to James this morning as it happens. I know you don't like him, but he's coming to the New Year's party with me, so please be nice to him." My cheeks feel hot as I finish speaking and wait for his response, slightly avoiding eye contact as I do so.

"You're bringing him?" he sounds quite hurt.

"Yes."

"But I told you, I thought you were over that, Soph. Babe, you can do better."

I shift from one foot to the other and nervously pick at my fingernails as I try to think up a defence. Honestly, he always makes me feel guilty even when I haven't done anything wrong.

"Are you bringing Chloe?"

"Of course I am."

Ha! Got him. God he's a hypocrite, I mean, okay, so I haven't actually told him specifically that I hate her because I love him and she's the skinny little perfect rich girl in the way, with the most annoying laugh ever. But he should know how I feel about her. I mean, I know I'm a good actress, but I'm not that good.

"Exactly."

"What do you mean, exactly?" he asks, looking slightly bemused.

"You can bring your girlfriend but I'm supposed to go on my own again and stand like a loser in the corner?"

"You weren't alone last year," he argues.

"Yes I was," I say rather too loudly, as half the office turns to look at me, but I can't help it, he's really pissed me off now. He just expects me to be alone forever.

"I'm sorry," he says quietly, looking embarrassed.

"Look, whatever you think of him, Dan, you have Chloe and I will not be alone at every party. So he's coming and you'd better be nice to him or our friendship will hit a big problem." I thought that was quite a good speech, even if the last bit didn't exactly make all that much sense. Before he gets the chance to answer, I storm over to my desk and, after sitting in angry silence for an hour or two, decide that I'm not getting any work done anyway so I might as well have an early lunch. Grabbing my bag, I head out, ignoring Dan as he says something to me and accidentally hit Barry on the head with my bag as I throw it over my shoulder.

"Ouch," he yells in mock pain, as my cheeks burn again.

"Sorry, Barry," I shout, as I start running towards the lift. "I'll buy you a muffin to make up for it."

* * *

Wandering back into TopShop, for the first time in months actually, the sheer size of it takes my breath away every time, literally. I have never found somewhere as exciting as this; I mean I know I love Harrods and Macys and Saks, but they don't have the TopShop sales, which means I can actually afford to buy the stuff in here. I do, however, have to make sure I'm careful with my time. Oh no, I don't! Marie's not in, besides it's only just been Christmas and the sales are on. I mean, how can they seriously expect me to fit all five floors into one hour? It just can't be done! I'll just work through tomorrow's lunch hour or something. Wandering around, I start picking things up and shoving them into my basket – a few presents for next year and a couple of tops, oh and that pair of shorts, and those dungarees are hot, I'll have them. Now for the shoes. Oh my God, they are perfect! I stand transfixed in the middle of the shoe display, staring open-mouthed at the perfect pair of shoes to wear to Ruth's wedding. I'm so excited. Me, the maid of honour! Okay, so I don't exactly know what it is I have to do, but I do know that I get to wear this amazing dress: it's floor-length with little spaghetti straps and a low back, in the most beautiful deep red. Granted, red isn't the colour best suited to my skin type, but I love it and I have just found the perfect shoes. A long thin heel that looks like it's wrapped in red silk and little straps wrapping round the ankles and lying delicately across the toes. Fair enough, the chances of my being able to walk in them are slim to none, but they look so gorgeous and the colour is exactly the same as the dress – it's fate.

"Sophie, hello." The shop assistant strolls up to me cheerfully.

"Hello, Kerri, busy day?"

"Not really, which ones are you buying today?"

I point at the stunning shoes, grinning.

"Those please."

"Okay, I'll just bring out your size. Have a seat."

Walking towards the shoe display I sit down, thinking about how good the shoes are going to look when I have them on. I love this place; I mean, not only do they know my name but my shoe size too. I don't even have to ask sometimes, they just bring out the new ones they've got that they think I'll like.

"Here you go," she smiles, as she walks towards me holding out the box.

"Thanks," I say, glancing at my watch. "I don't need to try them on, I'll just buy them." I stand by the till holding out my card to her, itching for her to hurry up so that I will actually own these amazing shoes.

Stepping out into the cold January wind, I pull my coat closer around me and reach for my phone. I excitedly dial Ruth's number and wait for her to answer.

"Ruth Jones speaking."

"Hey."

"Oh hey, you alright?"

"Yeah, just out for a bit of retail therapy. Guess what?" I say, my voice higher than usual with excitement.

"Erm… my 'Ruthcatra, one hundred and one ways to make babies' has been published in your magazine?"

"No, that's next month," I laugh, as I weave between the people hording towards me. "So guess what I've found?"

"What?"

"I have just found the perfect pair of shoes to go with the dress for your wedding."

"Really?" she doesn't sound that interested.

All these years and I still haven't managed to make her see the importance of shoes. Pausing at the little vendor on the corner of the street where my office is, I perch my phone between my ear and shoulder as I pay him for a large chocolate muffin, Barry's 'sorry for hitting you on the head with my bag' present – he gets about one of those a week on average.

"Yes, they're amazing, so hot, you'll fall in love with them," I say, as I wave at the man and walk down the road again, rearranging my bags.

"As long as they match, it's all good with me."

"Well they do, and they look fantastic." So I haven't actually tried them on yet, but they will look amazing, I know they will.

"Okay, well I had better be getting back to work. Oh, where are we meeting for coffee next week?"

"On the corner by that new Chinese restaurant, down Bath Road."

"The corner? Look how many times do I have to tell you that the whole prostitution thing was just to tide me over for a few months, that life is over now!"

"Oh come on, one last night of work as a free woman." I'm starting to giggle uncontrollably as I walk through the front doors of my building and wave at Mandy, the receptionist.

"Okay then, but we have to split the old ones."

"But you love the old blokes," I stutter, trying to get my breathing back to normal.

"Well I know, but they're going to have to get used to you, you are taking over my side of the business, you know."

"I'm going to be exhausted." My face is starting to ache from laughing so much.

"You'd better get some rest then," she giggles. "I'll see you at the fitting on Thursday night."

"Oh I forgot about that, yeah. What time is it, seven at yours?"

"Yeah that's right, bye, Soph."

"See you later, babe." Hanging up the phone, I give a final little giggle and head back to my desk, placing my beautiful new shoes in the 'shopping drawer' of my desk. It's actually a really good idea I had, to keep one drawer of my desk free to put in the stuff I buy at lunchtimes. It may mean I have extra piles of paper lying around, making my desk look slightly messier than some of the others – except Sandra's, hers is a tip, and she doesn't even have a shopping drawer – but at least my new purchases are kept safe.

Now my computer is fixed at home, after writing a few notes, I email myself some information so I can get it when I'm home. Well to tell you the truth, it was never really broken, but there's a man down the road who fixes them and he is very hot. So I may have asked him to come and look at it, knowing full well it was fine. I then email a couple of people for interviews, which I thought might give a nice spin on the Valentine's Day article.

I resist the urge to check my Facebook page again and instead decide to marvel over the fact that I, Sophie Farrier, have a date, an actual date, with a real man, and not just any man, but with James! The closest thing I'll be getting to Orlando Bloom, for at least the next few years. I'll have to leave early today and get Emily to meet me in town for some emergency shopping – a new outfit is mandatory when going on a first date with someone so hot they actually make women drool. After trying and failing to concentrate on some work for all of ten minutes, I grab my phone again and hurriedly scroll down to Emily's number, tapping my pen on my desk as I wait for her to answer.

"Bonjour."

"Em, you're never going to guess who I have a date with?" I squeak down the line.

"What? Who? Tell me everything," she squeals at me before hushing her voice. "Sorry, the curator just walked past and gave me a frown," she giggles.

"James."

"What, you mean 'sex on a stick' James from the reception and Christmas?"

"Yes, oh my God, Em, I nearly died! He just phoned out of the blue and was all like, 'I'm so sorry about Christmas, I was just feeling awkward and didn't know what to do, but I want to see you again if that's okay.'"

"What did you say?" she says, totally engrossed in my story.

"Well, I was just trying to be all cool and was like, 'I thought you were going back to LA', and he said that he couldn't get back until after New Year's. So I said 'Oh, what are you going to do for New Year's Eve then? I'm going to my office party,' and then he said, 'Well actually, I was going to ask if I could spend New Year's Eve with you'. So I said that maybe he could come with me to the party and then he said, 'Yeah, that would be amazing.'"
As I finish talking, I gasp for air and feel slightly lightheaded. I think that time, I may actually have genuinely starved my brain of oxygen for slightly too long.

"Really?" She doesn't believe me, the bloody cheek.

"Okay," I admit there is no point in lying to her as she knows me too well, "he was the cool one and I couldn't even move. I think I almost got money from tourists thinking I was a living statue." I can't help but giggle at the thought of myself standing there transfixed, and from what I can hear of the muffled giggles on the other end of the phone line, Emily is picturing the same thing.

"So I need to go emergency date-outfit shopping," I interject quickly.

"Oh yeah, of course. God, we haven't done that in ages."

"All right, rub it in," I feign annoyance at her for this

statement.

"Sorry, I just meant…"

"Yeah I know," I interrupt her. "So what say we finish early today and meet at the station at 3? That gives us a couple of hours."

"I don't know if I can get away that early, sweets."

"You have to, Em, that's what friends are for. You have to meet me, this is an emergency! I'm going out with a Hollywood hunk! Literally!" I stare at the phone as if to try and get my point across to her.

"Okay, but half three and no earlier, or I'll be for it."

"Okay, half-three then. Yay, I'm so excited! See you then, bye."

Hanging up the phone, I flick onto Google and search New Year's dresses, which comes up with nothing except a couple of nice dresses I could wear to work or on a normal night out, which I may accidentally have clicked on and bought. But nothing for the party, although at least I don't have to worry so much about my January wardrobe now, which is a weight off my shoulders. Tapping my fingers I wait impatiently for the time to pass so I can go shopping. Dan has made a couple of attempts to apologise to me, but despite the new shoes, I'm still too annoyed with him. Besides, it will do him good to get the silent treatment from me for a while, might show him what he's missing.

* * *

At last, grabbing my stuff, it's time to meet Emily. Thank God I have an excuse for these shoes and don't have to hide them, otherwise I think they would stretch my bag completely out shape. I make a hasty getaway from the office and practically jog, in a very slow teetering way, to the station, where I wait for the usual thirty minutes. That girl is always late, literally always, for everything, ever! I don't understand it. We've been sitting at home before and both been completely dressed and ready to go out, two hours before we are actually going out, and yet somehow, when the taxi turns up, she always manages to become suddenly busy with something, making us ten minutes late downstairs. The taxi-man has driven off more than once because I just couldn't get her downstairs on time.

"Hello," I can hear her voice carrying faintly over the crowds as I sit holding my coffee. Jumping up, I see her strolling towards me as if she's right on time, and I can't help giggling to myself no matter how many times I tell her she will always be late, but you have to kind of love her for it, except when she makes you miss a sale or the trailers at the cinema.

"Hey, babe. Right, let's go! We have exactly two hours to find the perfect outfit for a Hollywood date." I decided while I was drinking my coffee that taking on a managerial role on this shopping trip was the only way to get everything done. So I march off before she can reply and she hurries after me as I head straight for Gucci. Three minutes later, we emerge breathless from laughter and head for Dorothy Perkins.

"Six hundred pounds," she gasps. "It was a curtain from the fifties surely?" It is all I can do to nod my head in agreement, as tears of mirth stream down my face. I think maybe I got carried away with the whole Hollywood date idea, and am pretty sure the shop assistant was thinking the same. I thought I was looking pretty good today as well – maybe it was the laddered tights.

It's been over an hour and so far all we have both managed to buy are three or four pairs of shoes each, and Emily bought this gorgeous top in Zara, which was only ever to be worn by somebody as skinny as she is, but still, it's something I can keep in mind for once I finish my Special K diet. That reminds me, I was going to join that new gym. Right, Sophie, keep focused, I have to find my dress and I am running out of shops.

This is a disaster. I have ten minutes of shopping time left and I still haven't found the right outfit. Oh God, oh God, I have to look perfect, not just for James – I mean he has already seen me in my pyjamas at Christmas – but because Chloe will be there. Okay, last shop. I know, I know, if I had that problem in Gucci what the hell am I going into Dolce and Gabbana for, but the thing is, not only are they my last hope but they also have a sale on! Also, I did get a new credit card the other day, and I know my dad told me that I should never get one, and then never get a second or a third one, but it said all this stuff about interest free so I have to try it out and use it, don't I? Emily may also be looking at me sceptically, but as soon as we walk through the door we rush to the racks of beautiful dresses. Okay this is it, I can feel it, I will find my perfect dress in here. Picking up an armful of dresses I head for the fitting rooms, leaving Emily on the plush armchair outside sneakily trying to drink her orange juice without anyone noticing.

Pulling the silky black material over my head and feeling it against my skin, I just know this is the dress: a floor-length black silk dress with a back that plunges right down to the very base of my spine, with delicate laces of diamonds stretching across my back and up to the straps holding it in place. God, I could just stand here and look at my back all day, I look amazing. And bloody hell, I look just as good from the front, with a plunging neckline revealing just enough. I am actually welling up, I've never looked so sexy, and I've just realised I already have the perfect shoes in my secret shoebox. Opening the curtain, I step out and see Emily's mouth drop open immediately.

"Oh my God!" Yes, yes, yes, I knew I looked fantastic, this is so my dress. "You look amazing, Soph, really breathtaking."

"I know." I can't help beaming as I spin round, enjoying the feeling of the beautiful material as it swept against my legs. "I have to buy it now."

"How much is it?"

"I have no idea." Who cares how much it is? I'll sell my car if I have to. Picking up the price tag I gulp inwardly… I might have to sell my car. Okay, it's fine, I can use my new credit card that has a limit of eight hundred pounds on it, then I'll just put two hundred on the other card, yeah, that's perfect. I have interest free on that one anyway so it's totally worth it. Walking up to the till by some miracle I manage to avoid letting Emily see how much it is and just say 'enough' whenever she asks me. After all, it's my birthday in a few months, so I'm sure I can pay it off with some of the money I get for that.

I practically skip all the way home. This is the nicest thing I have ever bought. It's just amazing. I love it, I love it, I really, really love it. Hanging it on the door of my wardrobe, I sink down onto my bed and just stare at it for a while. I honestly think this is one of the happiest moments of my life.

Chapter Fifteen
The big night – will I make it to midnight?

Saturday, I can't believe it's here already – New Year's Eve and the big day. This better go well, because as of midnight I only have one year to find a man and get married. I have a list of ambitions and general life things I want to do, which I wrote in my first year of uni as a task in one of my lectures, except I took it really seriously and so have stuck to it. Okay, so there are a couple of things on there which I have since had to cross off due to unseen circumstances, like going to Australia for a year, but I have amended that and am hoping to be sent there soon for work, so I can cross it off my list then. But the most serious item on the list is to be married by the year two thousand and ten, so that gives me a year. But I have faith in my dress and shoes, and I also have faith in my nail technician and hairdresser, who I am visiting this morning in about... twenty minutes, bugger.

Jumping up, I throw on a pair of jogging bottoms, a hoodie and a cap, run out of the house and promptly return to pick up my purse so I can at least pay them for beautifying me. I love going out in old jogging bottoms and a cap, it always makes me feel a little bit like a celebrity hiding from the press. Just the thing, because if tonight goes well I might actually be a celebrity wife hiding from the press in Hollywood before long.

Bloody hell, I didn't even think about that. If I marry James I'll get to cross three things off the list at once: married, famous and living in Hollywood. It may be true that he's not actually properly famous yet, but I Googled him the other night after he asked me out and apparently, he's up and coming and going to be the new Steven Spielberg, which has to be good, and his next film is going to be massive. There is even talk of him being a new heartthrob and appearing in a film or two! How exciting is that! I still think I'm dreaming, I really do. All week I have been expecting someone to pinch me and I'll wake up to reality, but no, this really is happening, and on top of everything I was talking to Emily the other night and apparently, she reckons Dan is jealous, which means that I have two men after me. Those shoes seriously are actually magic. They're even better than those cute little red ones that Dorothy wears in the Wizard of Oz that transport her home.

* * *

He's late. I can't believe it. I've been sitting here for nearly ten minutes already and he's not here. My hands are shaking and I feel slightly sick as the time ticks by agonisingly slowly. He had better not have stood me up. If he has that really is it for his chances with me. Oh God, if he has I'll never live it down. Dan will go on forever. I can't believe the bastard.

"Soph," Emily calls from the hallway,

"Yeah?" I say dejectedly, and then making the sudden decision to rant to her, "He's stood me up, Em, the bastard. I knew he was a twat from the word go, but no, I thought that just because he was gorgeous I would give him… oh hi." Shit! Okay, so this is awkward. James is standing in front of me grinning wickedly, and I suddenly notice he has the same cheeky glint in his eye that Dan has when he gains access to information he can torment me with.

"Hi, Sophie, sorry I'm late, got caught in traffic," he smiles.

"That's okay, I was just erm… shall we go?" I start to usher him into the hallway as I shoot daggers at Emily, who is practically crying with silent laughter. Well that wasn't exactly the romantic moment I had envisaged, in actual fact, I think it had to be on a par with that dinner in Rome. As we reach the door he starts leaning towards me. What is he doing? Don't tell me I have something stuck to my face or something now.

"You look beautiful," he whispers, and then kisses me on the cheek.

Bloody hell, I wasn't expecting that. I can feel myself grinning like a moron but I don't care, he just made up for the last fifteen minutes. I mean, I actually think that apart from his timekeeping abilities, which I clearly need to work on with him, this man may be perfect! This is going to be the best night ever!

Pulling up to the building, the butterflies in my stomach start to make me feel as if I'm at the end of a runway about to take off. His car is making me feel like a film star as we turn into the car park, the tinted windows preventing anyone from seeing who is inside, but I can see everyone admiring it as I check out their outfits. Oh, Jessica from human resources scrubs up well. Who would have thought that a pair of legs like that was hidden under all those trousers she wears? And bloody hell, Kevin looks almost hot! A tuxedo really is like some sort of magic cloak that transforms any man into a presentable creature, although he definitely must have some sort of make-up on those spots because there is no way that a tuxedo can clear up your skin as well. At least I'm pretty sure it can't, unless you get an actual magic one. Getting out of the car takes me about ten minutes because I have a habit of falling out of them. Not on purpose or anything you understand, but I guess cars just don't like me that much. In fact, my nickname used to be 'Sophie-fall-over'. I got that one after I fell out of a car at my friend's thirteenth birthday in front of everybody, with my skirt over my head and granny knickers on show, and I'm determined that I won't have a repeat of that tonight.

Once out of the car we make our way to the lift and up into the office. My legs are beginning to shake and I can feel the anticipation rising, except I don't really know why. I mean, I know Dan will be there with his girlfriend, but it's not like I haven't seen them together before and I know that James will be a hit with everyone. I mean he's charming, clever, interesting and absolutely gorgeous. Maybe it's my dress. No, I know I look good. This dress is amazing – it should be for the price. Hmm, maybe it's… oh I don't know, I'll figure it out later. All this thinking is making me frown and that won't do my look any good.

Wow, this is actually going okay, everyone has commented on how good I look and all the girls have come up to me asking about James. Although Chloe does look stunning, I have caught Dan looking over at me a few times even if he hasn't come over to say hello yet. James is getting on with everyone and entertaining people with stories of his time in Hollywood. He really is incredible, and I can feel myself beaming every time I think about how good we must look tonight and how jealous all the women in the office are.

"Hi, Sophie."

"Oh, hey, Dan. I didn't see you there." That's a lie, I had seen him walking over as soon as he started moving and had turned away, pretending to be busy eating an hors d'oeuvre, which I decided was the most disgusting thing ever to enter my mouth and nearly gagged in public, as Tracey from accounting gave me a look of mingled amusement and astonishment.

"You look lovely," Chloe pipes up in her annoying posh squeaky voice, as I try to smile graciously, "really elegant, doesn't she, Dan?"

What the bloody hell is that supposed to mean? That I normally look like an oversized hippo in a glass museum? I look at Dan, waiting for his response.

"Yeah, you look stunning," he mumbles, meeting my eyes for a second before looking briefly at my boobs and then over at something on the other side of the room. Yes, I knew it. He so wants me. You may be rich, pretty, skinny and posh, Chloe, but have you got my boobs or personality? Ha!

"Thanks," I reply in a slightly more refined tone than usual, glancing around for James to come and rescue me before she starts talking to me again. I can't handle another conversation with this woman, it may tip me over the edge and force me to ruin a perfectly good pair of shoes beating her to death with the heels. But James is nowhere to be found. Busy telling his stories to a bunch of gushing women and men no doubt. Damn.

* * *

Two hours later and I have been wandering around on my own like a lemon talking to people I barely know, and worse, people I don't really like, with them all asking, 'Where's that man you're with?' or 'Who's that handsome bloke of yours? I'd like to meet him, bring him over'. And me just standing there shrugging and looking like a complete and utter moron, just saying, 'Erm, I don't know, sorry!' Honestly, men, they need leads on them or they just run off and get lost sniffing for the nearest short skirt like a dog on heat. I spot him out the corner of my eye looking slightly red in the cheeks, as he comes strolling out of the lift. I walk over as quickly as I can without causing too much attention to be focused on me and because it would be physically impossible to run in these shoes even if I had wanted to. I read somewhere once that high heels were a male invention to make it harder for women to run away from them, and you know what, I really do think that's the truth. But, these shoes do make my legs look fantastic and they finish off my outfit perfectly. Anyway, I need to concentrate on finding out why the hell James just disappeared for two hours.

"James," I say slightly out of breath, trying to balance as I nearly fall into him.

"Sophie, sorry I had an important call I had to take." He looks genuinely sorry and there seems to be something else in his face, worry maybe.

"What's wrong, was it bad news?" I ask, suddenly worried.

"No, not really, but I have to fly out first thing in the morning."

"Oh," I try not to sound disappointed. I mean, it's not like I wanted him to come home with me or anything but, I don't know, it might have been nice if he had come in for some coffee or just not to be on such a tight timescale.

"Sorry, Sophie, but are you ready to leave?"

"Oh right, yes. Sorry, yes. Let's go." Glancing behind me, I see Dan looking directly at me as he stands talking to some of the boys from research with Chloe hanging off his arm. I half smile at him before turning back to James and clasping his outstretched hand as we walk towards the door. To be honest I can't lie about the fact that I'm not overly depressed to be leaving. My feet were starting to hurt, and by starting to hurt I mean I think my feet may now be deformed for life, like my toes have actually all broken.

* * *

As the car comes to a stop at the front of my building I open my eyes. Shit, I've been asleep for practically the whole journey home. I hope I didn't snore. Cautiously, I turn my head slowly to see the look on his face. He smiles at me, resting his head back against the seat.

"I guess I should go then," I say, yawning slightly and smiling back at him.

"Yeah, I suppose so," he replies, looking almost as if he doesn't really want me to go.

"I hope you don't have to drive to far. I mean if you have to leave early then, I don't know, I mean, you can always stay here." I can't meet his eyes as I wait for his reply.

"I… I don't know. Would you mind? I mean, I'd have to be up and out by seven."

His eyes are sparkling and his perfectly formed mouth is twitching slightly with a smile as he waits for my answer.

"No, I don't mind. I don't have to go, do I?" I laugh slightly as our eyes meet again.

"Okay then."

Walking up the stairs I can feel the butterflies rising in my stomach again as the anticipation starts to bubble. What should I do? I mean if he is going to be the 'one' then I should definitely not sleep with him. On the other hand, I have had a lot of champagne, he's the most handsome man I've ever had back to the flat and I may never see him again. Oh God, if only decisions like this were as easy as picking a pair of shoes to buy on my lunch break.

"I'm sorry we missed seeing the New Year in at the party," he says softly as we reach my front door.

"Oh that's okay, I didn't even notice," I gush, as I rummage around in my bag for my keys. Opening the door, I can already feel his hand on my hip as I push through and dump my bag on the table.

"So, happy New Year."

Turning round to face him as he says this I find our faces are inches apart. Oh my God, this is it. I'm about to kiss the hottest guy I've ever been this close to, without being insanely drunk and throwing up on them.

"Happy New Year," I say, leaning forwards a fraction. I close my eyes and part my lips and wait for what seems like forever for his to connect with mine. He strokes my face gently before holding it in his hands as his soft lips caress mine, sending shivers down my spine. Wow, he really is good at this! We start moving backwards towards my bedroom door. As I grapple for the handle, his hand reaches the small of my back while his other hand is again stroking my face. Oh God, that's not fair, everyone knows that if a man does that you automatically fall in love with them, which means I definitely have to stop what is about to happen.

Oh God, how am I supposed to stop this? I kind of still want it to happen but I know that I have to stop it if we are ever going to get married. Pulling away, I look up at him for a second before staring at my sore feet.

"I, I…" Bugger, what do I actually say?

"You're uncomfortable?" he says, slightly taken aback.

"No, it's not that, I just don't want to…"

"I should go."

Oh no, I've really gone and done it now. He's going to walk out of my flat and my life forever! I have to do something, so grabbing his arm as he turns to leave, I desperately try and think of something to say.

"James, I, it's not that I'm uncomfortable, I, I just, well I like you and I don't want to ruin anything, you know?" I hope that

148

made sense because I'm pretty sure I could have been speaking German from the way he's standing there gaping at me, and I think I may have just made a fool out of myself.

"Oh, right…" Great, now I've freaked him out. "… me too."

What did he just say? Did he actually just say that he liked me too? I must be dreaming, this cannot be real. After so many bad relationships – okay two bad relationships, but they were really, really disastrous – I have finally found someone amazing. I can't wait to tell Emily.

"So…" I say, wondering what happens now.

"Look, I'm going to go anyway. I still have to pack my things when I get back to my parents' house."

"Oh, ok," I say, glancing down at the floor briefly.

"Hey listen, go and get changed for bed and I'll bring you in a glass of water in a second," he grins, as he kisses me lightly on the cheek and makes his way in the direction of the kitchen.

I'm then left standing in the empty doorway sighing almost contentedly. I can't be completely content because I think my feet may be bleeding by this point, and so moving to my room as quickly as possible, I collapse on the bed and pull them off gingerly, trying not to cry out in pain at the swollen lumps that are now in the place where my feet used to be. Oww.

Hopping into bed I glance around, glad that I had at least tidied some of my room up the other day, and wait for James to return.

"Hey," he mutters, poking his head round the door and picking his way over to me, placing the water on my bedside table and perching next to me on the bed.

"Thanks," I smile.

"Anytime," he laughs softly, placing a hand on the side of my face and kissing me again. "I have to go but I'll call you soon, okay?" he says, his face inches from mine, his hand still stroking my hair gently.

"Okay, I… I, thank you for tonight, and I'll be waiting for you to phone," I practically whisper.

"Good night, beautiful," he says at last, pulling the cover further up over me and kissing me on the forehead before leaving the room.

Well that was definitely the most romantic thing to ever happen to me!

Chapter Sixteen
Hens gossiping and giggling

I cannot believe it, Ruth's getting married tomorrow. I remember like it was yesterday when we were all still in school, drinking fizzy water with everything we could find poured into it to try and make ourselves hyper. She hadn't wanted a big hen night so we had decided that tonight we would have a big girlie sleepover, just like old times, and talk about everything we've done. I hope it will give me some inspiration too, because I've hit a bit of writer's block as far as my speech is concerned. Not that anyone knows. I've even told Emily that I finished it ages ago. Gathering up several bags between us, Emily and I rush out to the car and over to Ruth's house, where we find her husband-to-be, Darren, being ushered out by the rest of the group – we're late as usual. Getting inside, however, my excitement bubbles over as I jump up and down, squealing like a twelve-year-old and hugging everyone in sight, and then I survey the dining room table. With our little hoard added, there must be at least fifteen bottles of wine and more sweets and crisps than I could possibly imagine. This is going to be so exciting, a proper catch-up. Okay, so I know that we're supposed to be talking about Ruth and her wedding and everything, but let's face it, the whole of tomorrow is basically going to revolve around her and I have a massive love triangle problem going on that I need to talk through.

"So girlies, I have a dilemma for you," I almost shout over the chattering and giggling. A hushed silence ensues almost immediately as they all turn and face me with expressions that show the clear love of gossip they all share with me.

"Gossip, I love it, tell me all!" Kate yelps, pulling me down onto the floor where there is an array of cushions, blankets and beanbags ready for our night.

"It's not gossip exactly, more a personal problem."

"Yeah right," comes Tanya's voice from behind me, as she sits down with a bag of crisps in one hand, radio in the other.

"Did you not get the night off, babe?" I say to her, pointing towards the police radio in her hand.

"Oh yeah, I just keep it with me just in case," she smiles. "Don't you worry, I'll still be on the wine with the rest of you."

Looking around I suddenly notice that there's someone missing.

"Where's Becca?" I ask, finally figuring out who it was.

"Still at work, she'll be here soon, and enough of this changing the subject, tell us all, every little detail," says Ruth, plonking herself down in front of me as she begins to munch on a bowl of strawberry laces, always her favourite sweet. I had nearly bought her a year's supply, but Emily stopped me and we went halves on a selection of trinkets for her, all put in a special wedding box. Anyway, better get on with it and finally sort out which bloke to go for. I glance at Emily as she gives me a slightly withering look – mind you, she has heard this story about forty times already – and then grabs the biggest bar of chocolate she can find and settles down to text Sam on her phone.

"Okay, so basically it's Dan or James…" I begin.

* * *

Oh my God, it's five a.m. in the morning and today one of my best friends will be getting married. This is massive. Not only is this just the second wedding I will ever have been to, but she is the first of our group to tie the knot. There's about seven of us, and we were inseparable at school and have been ever since. Although we have all gone in different directions in our lives, we are still as close as ever. Last night we spent hours drinking cheap rosé wine and reminiscing over the past, and my present dilemmas, with me commenting every couple of minutes on how I can't believe she's finally taking the plunge. The two of us were quite a formidable duo back in the day, the dirtiest minds in the school – it was official, the ability to turn anything said into a dirty joke. But now here she was, all grown-up and about to get married, and I am maid of honour. That reminds me, I have to finish writing my speech before we start getting ready. But for the moment I think the thing I need most is coffee and lots of it. Standing up, I quickly fall back down again, my head swimming, and start giggling to myself as I sit there on Ruth's feet. She doesn't even stir. I might be a little pissed still, oops.

* * *

Two hours later and we are exactly two hours behind schedule, but at least we are all reasonably sober, I think. Ruth has her dress on and we are all sitting awaiting our hair and make-up. I am personally really hoping that they are able to do something with the bags that have appeared overnight like bin liners under my eyes. Whose silly idea was it to have a wedding start at nine in the morning when the bride and all her friends have clearly spent the night drinking? Thank God Darren had his stag do last week, otherwise I doubt he would ever have made it to the church.

Wow, my shoes look amazing. Really, really, really amazing. I know I have to wear the same dress as the other bridesmaids but I still have to stand out and be a little bit special. I mean, I am the maid of honor after all, aren't I, and these shoes are the things that set me apart from the crowd. Sure, everyone will be staring at Ruth's beautiful dress and at her most of the ceremony, it is her wedding after all, but they will definitely notice my shoes too. I can hear the whispers now, 'Look at her shoes, they're amazing, she looks so good in them'. Spinning around I nearly overbalance, but stop myself by grabbing the bedpost. Checking my reflection one last time, I walk into the next room ready for the gasps of envy at my beautiful shoes.

"You know you'll never be able to walk in those, right?" says Becca as soon as I enter.

Why does everyone say that? I mean granted, it took Emily slightly longer because for the first ten minutes she was stuttering over their beauty, which I admit was my desired reaction, but eventually she had said exactly the same.

"And you will never be able to stand for long in them, will you?" pipes up Sarah, staring down at the silky deep-red colour that wrapped itself around my ankles and toes.

"Well that doesn't matter, does it? I mean as soon as I get to the reception they come off and those little red dolly shoes I bought go on ready for the dancing," I laugh, as I teeter over to the make-up table and add yet more bronzer.

Chapter Seventeen
Wedding Time

This is so beautiful, I'm definitely going to make it my life's work to attend as many weddings as I can now, just to make sure that I have enough inside knowledge to make my own perfect. The ceremony is lovely. I mean, I do get a little distracted during the main talking bit, but the whole 'you may kiss the bride' is so lovely, and just like Darius from Pop Idol or X Factor or wherever used to say, 'you can really feel the love' in the church. Then everyone is clapping and crying as they walk back down the aisle together.

The church is small and intimate, a small village church with an archway over the path leading up to the front entrance, which has been covered in white roses and ivy. At the back of the church is a small copse of trees, which makes the perfect backdrop for the photographs of the wedding party. I can quite honestly say that whilst Harry's wedding was huge and stunningly extravagant, this is just perfect – completely different but absolutely beautiful. The guests are mainly family and close friends, and we have a few photos taken of everybody lined up against the side of the church.

I think it is made all the more stunning for me because I had helped pick her dress. It does look perfect on her – an ivory masterpiece – and we got it cheap because I got the girl in the store to trade discount for shoe advice.

As we reach the hotel where the reception is being held, I catch sight of it from behind and admire the detail on the bodice: corseted and completely encrusted with tiny jewels, which, when you looked closely, were all in the pattern of roses, tiny perfect roses, all over it. The skirt of the dress had seven layers and was gathered up into shorter layers at one side, giving the whole dress volume. Standing next to her groom in the doorway of the hall where we would be eating dinner to greet people, the pink and white roses interwoven with ivy that are decorating the entrance make her look even more beautiful. Entering the hall for the first time since I helped her pick out all the decorations, I gasp in awe at the wonder of the place. It looks like an enchanted forest, or a fairy garden or something equally as wondrous. The tables are covered in long white tablecloths with large centrepieces, which continued the theme of the roses and the ivy but with different colours on each table. The head table had white roses, the others red or yellow or pink, and the ceiling seemed to be twinkling as a blanket of fairy lights gave the appearance of being under the stars.

Perhaps I should be a personal shopper or something, or

an events-organiser-come-interior-decorator – I'll have to add that to my list of future jobs. It's amazing really that I didn't think about coming to weddings much before, I mean they're really quite fun, the alcohol flowing, and it's amazing how many drinks they have behind that bar, it's more stocked than most clubs, amazing. There are loads of blokes around drinking and looking good, because they are all wearing suits. It's really easy to tell which ones are single aswell, or almost single, because they don't have emotional girlfriends hanging on to them. That's the other great thing, if you're not emotional you end up looking great because loads of the other girls are balling their eyes out and ruining their make up. Huh, I never even thought about it but this might be an even better place to find a bloke than the airport. Okay I'll admit that when the boys did their speeches I may have got a tiny, miniscule bit emotional, especially when Darren sang her a song, even though it was terrible, but you could just tell how much he loved her, it was so sweet. I might have to throw a joke into my speech about it, not that I can remember what song it was but I still haven't technically finished the speech, and I was looking for inspiration to help me wing it.

* * *

Oh God, speech time, here it goes. With a gulp I stand up and open my mouth to start speaking.

"Okay, so I guess this means it's time for me to start talking. What can I say though? I know, everybody gasp, I'm almost lost for words… almost!" Pause for laugh. Come on people, laugh.

Okay, I'll settle for the slight snigger, this is a tough crowd. I'm more nervous than that time I had to give a presentation of my work to Marie at the office.

"I know it's not exactly normal for the maid of honour to make a speech, but hey, I am because there are a few things that need to be said. Besides, I can't let the boys have all the fun, can I? Although the song was beautiful, Darren, it wouldn't win you X Factor." Wow, that one actually got a laugh, they're easing up. "Ruth, you look so glamorous… There was a time some of us wondered if the glamorous days would ever arrive, after that trip down the motorway with your underwear hanging out the window. Mind you, I think that could have been your first love when we pulled that 'man in a van' along the M25." People are actually laughing properly now, the wine is clearly taking effect, that or I must be funnier than I thought. That will show Dan that he's been lying to me for all these years. Oh shit, in the middle of a speech, stop daydreaming, Sophie.

"Anyway," I recover with only a slight burning in my face, "I'm glad you didn't take up the offer of proposal from that Turkish bloke on holiday a few years ago, because to tell you the truth, we didn't think he quite matched you. But Nick, I mean Darren…" FUCK! fuck, fuck! I cannot believe that I just called him the wrong name at her wedding, she is going to kill me! I just said his name right about two minutes ago as well, how did I get it wrong? "… appears to be the perfect fit for you and well, I just wanted to say, I hope you have a wonderful happily ever after." There is scattered applause as I finish and sink back into my chair, trying to avoid looking at Ruth in the eye as Emily's uncontrollable giggling at my slip-up seems to be catching. I can't see my face but I can feel it, and it feels like it's on fire. I swear right now never to drink again, or at least after I've drunk away the memory of this disaster. Okay, well I'm never going to get pissed before making a speech again. Ever!

"Sophie." Oh bugger, here she comes, what am I going to say to her?

"Ruth, hey, beautiful meal by the way, you must give me the name of your caterer." That sounded good, I'm always hearing people say that on TV, although I can't say she looks as pleased as they usually do.

"Nick!" she says, glaring at me.

"I, erm, I got a bit confused," I say stupidly.

"Confused? I haven't even seen Nick for over two years!" she fumes, and I can feel my face reddening once again as a few guests begin to turn round and stare.

"I know, I was just so excited and you looked so beautiful, and I wasn't really thinking about Darren, no offence, lovely bloke, but I was more worried about talking about you." Now I'm babbling like a complete loony. I am so glad Dan isn't here to once again witness me being an idiot. Okay, now she's looking like she wants to punch me. Oh shit, I can't deal with this, she'll ruin her dress. Why did anyone trust me to make a speech? Think, Sophie... what shall I do? Somebody come and rescue me quick... no? Okay then, I'll have to deal with it myself.

"The band's really good," I say, attempting to change the subject again.

"I will kill you for this, you know," she says.

"I don't think anyone really noticed," I lie, "and I promise not to talk to anyone else all night, promise. And I'll buy you an extra present, and oh look, have a glass of wine."

She takes a huge gulp and breathes in deeply. "You never can let things run smoothly, can you?" she says almost smiling, but still pretty annoyed.

"Anyway, I've decided to pick a bloke depending on what happens in Paris next week," I say, attempting to change the subject and make her forget that I just said her ex-boyfriend's name instead of her actual husband's.

"Really?" She still doesn't look like she will let me get away from this spot without a black eye. Please, Fairy Godmother person, give me a distraction. I promise to be better if you help me out – I'll get you a great deal on shoes or sandals or something.

"And now it's time for the father/daughter dance. Clear the dance floor please." The DJ's voice fills me with relief as Ruth runs off to join her dad on the dance floor.

I knew I had a Fairy Godmother out there somewhere; I am so going to be on the lookout for her perfect shoes now. That way, at least I have a conversation starter when I next need her to help me out.

*   *   *

The rest of the evening manages to go by pretty smoothly, with me dodging Ruth and Darren at every possible interval, but I'm glad when we finally leave. That was honestly the most emotionally exhausting day I have ever spent, even worse than that time there was that sale at Zara, when I had to queue up from five in the morning and then fight this woman to get the pair of shoes I had lusted over for three weeks.

Emily seems to have enjoyed herself, and although it's been four hours since my tiny faux pas, she is still giggling like a small child as we sit in the cab on the way home, stolen champagne and food in hand.

Chapter Eighteen
Knocking down bridges

I'm so excited! I know I've been to Paris before, okay, like ten times in all, but I love it and it is the city of romance after all. More romantic than bloody Rome, but the less I think about that disaster the better. Dan has been in a surprisingly 'nice' mood recently. He didn't even take the piss that much about Ruth's wedding, despite the video somehow managing to find its way onto YouTube under 'The worst maid of honour ever', which I thought was a little harsh to be honest. Also, he still hasn't forwarded the link to everyone he knows, which is shocking because usually that would have been done as soon as he'd found out, with the added extra of the photos pinned to every bloody noticeboard in the office. I remember once when we were scuba-diving in Turkey, he shouted at me to pose as I was trying to pull on my stupidly small wetsuit (which was extra tight because I might have slightly underestimated my real size) and as I spun round to stop him, I fell off the edge of the boat… The picture reappeared on the noticeboard, after I had taken it down, every day for a month, until I tripped over and ripped my trousers in Berlin, and then that picture became the favourite for a long time!

Bugger, I've spent too long daydreaming and let Sam sneak into the bathroom before me… again. His shower's broken apparently. How a bloke who earns that much – not that I know what he earns, but I'm guessing from the clothes he wears and the car he drives that he earns a lot – lets his shower break and then doesn't fix it for over three weeks is beyond me. Personally, I think he's just keeping an eye on Emily – their relationship status has gone back to just boyfriend/girlfriend again. Standing outside the bathroom door I clear my throat loudly, hoping he can hear me over the sound of the shower and get the hint.

Ten minutes later I'm still standing in the same spot; I don't think he quite got the hint. Oh wait, just a minute, that's Emily's voice! I open my mouth to yell through the door at her. Hang on though, my God, that's Sam's voice! What's he saying? Oh that's disgusting! It is definitely way too early for me to have been subjected to that! I suddenly don't feel like breakfast, well maybe just a coffee, and a biscuit, or two, and maybe a piece of toast. So, giving the bathroom door my best look of disgust, I shuffle off to the kitchen and attempt to find a clean mug. We really need to draw up a new cleaning rota.

"Hi, Soph," Emily smiles at me, as she strolls into the room wrapped in a towel.

"You alright?" I reply with a cheeky grin crossing my face. I love taking the mick out of her 'extracurricular activities'.

"Yeah. Why?"

"Just never pegged you for such a morning person." She stops mid reach for the coffee, guessing what I meant.

"Oh God, Soph, you didn't... I thought we were being quiet... Did you have your ear up against the door?"

"No, you pervert, of course I bloody didn't, it was hard not to hear! I was just waiting to go in the shower, I need to do a lot of preparing ready for tonight." I look at her to emphasise this statement until, just when I start to think that my face is going to freeze into this expression, she catches on.

"Oh, of course! Paris!"

"Yep!" I squeal with excitement.

"So, have you decided what to wear yet?"

"No idea, I need your help."

"Today? Sweetheart, I can't!" What did she just say?

"What?"

"Sam's taking me to that exhibition. Remember?"

"Well yeah, but..." I can't think of a good enough reason for her to miss the exhibition for me, so I just give her what I think is my most pleading look.

However, catching sight of myself in the mirror – yes I know, a mirror in the kitchen, but I like to have one in every room, that way I know I'm always looking my best – I look slightly constipated, so quickly change expression.

"I can't, but you'll be fine, trust me."

Trust her? Okay, I need a vodka, or maybe not, I think it might be a bit early, even for me. I can't believe she's leaving me.

"But who am I going to consult about my wardrobe?" I whine.

"I thought we had already decided on the suitcase and it was just today's outfit?"

"Yeah, well I kind of had a last-minute rethink and decided I really needed to take that pair of satin blue lace-up stilettos I bought last Christmas, because I haven't really had a chance to wear them yet and I bought that handbag that matches them perfectly. So I now need to pack a whole new load of stuff that matches that theme." I gasp for breath when I finally finish my explanation, hoping that the fact I had said it so fast meant she hadn't understood me.

"You're repacking an entire suitcase to coordinate with one pair of shoes?" She's looking at me in that odd way again.

"Colour coordination is very important," I reply, trying to sound as snooty as possible.

"You are totally beyond me sometimes," she smiles incredulously, as she shakes her head and wanders back into her bedroom with her coffee.

"Yeah well… I just want to make sure I look hot," I call after her in a last ditch attempt to justify myself.

"You will," she calls back as the door shuts behind her. Well I knew I kept her around for something. She can sometimes, on very rare occasions, not terrify me with a 'fine' at the last minute. She can sometimes really come through for me. I feel a warm glow start to spread as I head back towards the shower so I can start getting ready, since by now I only have about eight hours left before Dan picks me up. Okay then, organisation. Shit! I can't do organisation. Never has been a strong point of mine. I'll try priorities, yeah I can do that. Okay then, priority number one is looking good, so that means the first thing to do is shower. Now, I have my towel, I have my phone, can't shower without music, and my new Herbal Essences shampoo and conditioner – I muse over whether this one will really make me act like the women in the adverts?

So the advert is a lie, which leaves me with yet another letter to write to the authorities of all things hair and make-up related. Glancing at the little digital display on my clock I see that I now have only exactly seven hours until Dan picks me up! I know I said that I was going to base my opinion on which man to go for (I know, me having a choice between two men, neither of whom is married, is amazing!), but the thing is I think I've already made up my mind. Dan has been so nice recently, and after everything that happened I think we may have a real chance, so I would be stupid to turn down the lust of my life for a dream man who hasn't contacted me since he went back to America. Plus, I got a rose this morning with an anonymous card, which said 'In preparation for your Valentine's Day trip, I wish I could be with you now but I can't, so I hope this will do until then', so it must be Dan that sent it because James doesn't even know that I'm going anywhere! I don't think he does anyway…

*   *   *

Five hours later and I have finally finished packing the perfect bag for a French trip. I have decided to use my matching black suitcase and vanity bag – very sophisticated. I bought them last year for my weekend away with my 'ex', Andy. He told me we

167

were going for a romantic weekend away, so getting excited I rushed out and decked myself out with everything I could find to make me look sophisticated and sexy, until we got there and his idea of romance was two nights in a Travelodge and a trek over a dirt track to get to a smelly pub that was showing the rugby. Needless to say, I came home on the Sunday and saw him for the last time on the Monday. Anyway, all that means is I had two new pieces of luggage, and about three hundred pounds worth of posh but sexy clothes that I haven't even had the chance to wear yet. My hair is still in curlers and I am just about to apply my make-up for the twentieth time – it really isn't going well today, which is beginning to annoy me a little – so making sure I am breathing steadily and after taking a large gulp of wine – straight out of the bottle because I was starting to panic and couldn't find a clean glass or the new cleaning rota – I start once again to draw a thin black line of eyeliner across my top lids. Stepping back I admire my reflection, although I can't help thinking there is something wrong with what I am seeing. But dismissing it as just the wine talking, I totter into the kitchen to make myself a sandwich, partly because I don't want to eat much – well what I mean is, eat as much as usual in front of Dan, as I am going to be putting the 'moves' as it were on him (properly this time) – but also partly to try and sober myself up a little as I hadn't realised what a bottle of rosé can do to you on an empty, stressed-out stomach, and legs.

* * *

As I am peering out of the window a couple of hours later,

I watch Dan pull up towards the building, and as I pull myself back into the room I smack my head on the window frame, sending stars flying in front of my face and causing an involuntary scream to escape from my mouth. I can see him look up startled before I fall to the floor in a dizzy heap. Fuck, that hurt! Twenty seconds later there is a thumping on the front door.

"It's open," I call out feebly, still sitting on the floor of the living room rubbing the back of my head, when a pair of very white K-Swiss trainers appear in front of me. Looking up, I see a concerned looking Dan standing in front of me, although I can still see the laugh trying to escape from his lips as he stares at my crumpled state.

"Why are you wearing trainers?" I say in horror.

"Do you like them? They're new," he says looking proud. "Chloe bought them for me." Oh I might have bloody known she'd bought them! Trainers on a romantic weekend to Paris – it's sacrilege! I mean, here I am all posh and sophisticated – at least I will be once I get up off the carpet – and here he is looking like a slob in very expensive slobby clothes.

"You have proper clothes to wear once we get there though, right?" I ask, crossing my fingers.

"I have a couple of suits with me if that's what you mean," he says, perching on the arm of the chair and raising his eyebrows.

"Well, it's just that we are supposed to be going for the Valentine's experience, which means restaurants and other… stuff," I gesture, looking at him pointedly.

"God, you're worse than Chloe sometimes," he mutters in an irritated way before getting up and picking up my suitcase.

Worse than Chloe? The bloody cheek! I mean, fair enough

I would like to have her money and her boyfriend, and I might even get that wish soon if all goes to plan, but I have much better style! So there! (Keep telling yourself that, Soph!)

"You coming then?" he calls out from the door.

Huh, his concern lasted a long time. I could have concussion for all he knows!

"Yes, I'm ready, right let's go," I say flustered and in pain, as I rush out to the hallway.

"Nice hair," he laughs as he puts his hand on the door handle.

What does that mean? Did I mess it up when I hit my head? Glancing in the hall mirror I nearly scream again and my face instantly flushes red as I see the brightly coloured rollers sticking messily out of my hair. Pulling them out quickly, I try to recover myself slightly and march rather haughtily past him and down towards the car.

* * *

Reaching the airport, I am filled with the same anticipation as every other time. You would think that by now the novelty would have worn off slightly but it hasn't, and I've also discovered a way to make people enjoy airports more, at least if they like shopping. I was talking to this woman a couple of years ago and she was saying how she hated airports because they made her really nervous and stuff, and so I just said that she should think of them as another shopping centre, except they're better because you are technically on the brink of leaving the country and so any purchases made don't count because they are holiday buys.

Even though I mostly fly on business, the same rules apply!

I head straight for Borders to find myself a book that I will never get the chance to read but will look lovely on my ever-growing bookcase at home until I do. I feel that as a writer it is important to read a lot, or at least give the impression that I do by stocking my shelves with lots of impressive-looking books, which works until somebody asks me about one of them and I have to make up some excuse about it being fantastic but I haven't read it in years. Usually works too, except one time when I told a date that I loved this book but couldn't remember it in detail because I hadn't read it in years. Turns out it was a book he had written and it had only been published six months earlier!

After ten minutes of browsing I find a book all about Africa and decide to buy that, not only because I plan on going there one day, but also because it was on sale and because the cover was a beautiful deep-orange colour. Ten minutes later and I feel much better for having a new shopping bag in my hand. Heading for the perfume shop, however, I am grabbed by the arm and dragged to the check-in desk by a fed up-looking Dan. He never has got used to my airport shopping routines.

"I wanted to get some perfume," I say sulkily, crossing my arms and realising that I resemble a small child doing exactly the same thing so quickly uncross them again, straightening my jacket and avoiding Dan's eyes in case he, too, had noticed my very small mirror image in the queue next to us.

"We're late already and we need to check in," was his reply, as if that makes any difference to my need for perfume.

"But…"

"I'll buy you some bloody perfume in Paris, okay?"

Oh my God, he really does like me! I knew he was getting jealous of James at the New Year's party, and I may have mentioned that James might have gone to Ruth's wedding with me, even though he had already been back in America for over a week at that point. I can feel butterflies doing a dance in my stomach as I think about the next couple of days.

"Okay, oh and thanks for the rose by the way," I say lightly with a slight quiver in my voice.

"That's okay," is all he says, looking at me quizzically, as my voice may have come out in more of a squeak than anything else. He turns back towards the desk as the man calls us forward and we check our bags in, after I hold up the queue for ten minutes hunting around for my tweezers in my handbag and transferring them to my suitcase. I know! Tweezers in my handbag! But if you get stuck in traffic or notice a stray hair in the mirror you can get it quickly without walking around all day with a really long chin hair staring at everyone.

* * *

Paris! Stepping out of the airport and towards the taxi that Dan has waiting for us, I breathe in the air and a broad smile crosses my face. My chance to feel like I really am in 'Sex and the City' or something. Staring into the sky at the bright evening stars all my hopes seem like a real possibility, and glancing back down at Dan I can see him smiling at me as he holds open the taxi door. Okay, not smiling, gritting his teeth slightly against the cold as he is about to call me. I hadn't noticed how cold it was in my excitement, but now that I am walking towards the cab the bitter wind catches me off guard.

"Bollocks in hell, it's freezing," I say before I can stop myself, and that time he definitely smiled but I think it was more at me than with me. Getting in he puts his arm round me and rubs my shoulder with his hand. Okay, now this is getting really quite surreal. He is beginning to act like we are an actual couple. Hmm, there is something going on here – I should probably ask. On the other hand, though, I am sitting in the back of a cab with Dan Shore's arm round me… I think I may just ride this one out for a while before I open my big mouth and ruin it. I close my eyes for a second, my head suddenly beginning to hurt, and when I open them again we are coming to a halt outside the hotel. Trying to wake myself up I step out of the car, starting to rub my eyes before realising I have make-up on, which by now is halfway down my cheek. Catching sight of my reflection I look like I have either just been attacked or just got home from a very heavy night out with eyeliner down my face, skirt right up my arse, and how the hell did I manage to get a ladder in my tights? Grabbing at Dan's outstretched hand I notice that even though he is still dressed in jeans and trainers he still looks incredibly smart and good looking, compared to me anyway, although Emily's Sam has that shirt and he does look better in it than Dan, not that I would ever admit that out loud, except maybe to Emily, but I certainly wouldn't tell Dan…

* * *

I can't believe we are going back tonight, the last two days have been amazing! We have been sightseeing; we went up the

Eiffel Tower together and he wrapped his arms around me at the top of it as we stood there and stared out across Paris. It was possibly the single most romantic moment of my life. Then he took me out to dinner at this little restaurant opposite the Notre Dame Church, which was all lit up and looked so beautiful, and he made the waiter move us to the table with the best view and sat there staring into my eyes, telling me I looked beautiful. I've never felt like more of a princess in all my life. He hasn't spoken a single word about Chloe all weekend and hasn't even corrected people when they've assumed we are a couple – the only bad thing was the fact that he made me eat frogs' legs.

As I finish packing my stuff and after spritzing myself with some of my new perfume that Dan bought me, I head into the lobby where he is waiting for me and greets me with a warm smile and a kiss on the cheek. Okay, that's it. I just have to find out what is going on with all this parallel universe stuff! When did we suddenly become a couple?

"So…" I start, wondering exactly how I am supposed to word this.

"Yes?"

"Erm, thanks for the perfume." Okay so I bottled it, I just couldn't ask, I am much happier living in ignorance.

"That's alright, the company's paying," he says, and I smile for a second before what he has just said registers and my face freezes.

"What?"

"The company's paying," he repeats, as if that's an explanation I should understand.

"What do you mean the company's paying?" I ask again, my

voice rising ever so slightly.

"Well, I give them the bill and they pay me back for it, like they do with the flights and stuff," he explains in a very slow voice, as if I'm simple or something, which only succeeds in confusing me more and pissing me off too.

"I got that bit," I say just as slowly, "what I meant is, why are they paying?"

"Because it's an expense."

"Why?" Now he really is confusing me and I can feel my brow furrow, which is not good for my frown lines, so I am going to have to get some more cream when I get to the airport, which is annoying me too.

"Because it's all part of the assignment. Didn't you get the email?" Now he looks slightly perplexed.

"What email?"

"The one from Marie we got the day before we came."

"But Marie's on leave, what's she doing emailing us?" Stupid bloody woman – I swear she lives to make me look like an idiot. I bet she never even sent me an email, although at the back of my mind I do recall an email that I deleted because I thought it was just a memo about the trip…

"She wanted us to write the article from the point of view of a couple being away."

"But we always write like that."

"Yeah, but she wanted us to pretend that we were a couple and do all the couple things and then write it as a couples' getaway article – not opposing viewpoints…" he pauses and a slightly guilty look momentarily crosses his face. "Actually, maybe it was a phone call, I thought I'd told you."

Well that just makes no sense at all does it? The woman's a complete twit! How she got to be Editor is completely beyond me. Why would she phone him and not me, and how the fuck could he just forget to mention it to me?

"But that means I have to write my whole article again!" That'll teach me. The first time I actually do some proper work while away and write the complete first draft, and now it's completely useless and I have to do the whole thing again. And even worse, by the way I have just reacted to this piece of information, Dan has now figured out that I knew nothing about the whole 'pretending' thing and is now beginning to laugh a little too hysterically for my liking, which is totally unfair seeing as it is actually his fault. Why am I even blaming myself? He just admitted that he's led me on and he knew that he hadn't told me what Marie had told him. Oh my God, it has just dawned on me, I bet he did this on purpose. This is punishment for me bringing James to the New Year's party. Oh God, I hate him, how could he?

"So you thought I was actually coming onto you?" he manages between breaths.

"Well, you didn't have to pretend quite so well," I say, furious and very embarrassed. How the hell am I supposed to get out of this one without looking like too much of an idiot?

"I'm sorry but… but you knew about me and Chloe," he says, his laughter suddenly stopping.

"Oh yeah, because that's never stopped you before," I say, really angry with him now.

"I never led you on, Sophie."

"Yes, you did!"

"No, I didn't, we're friends!"

"So that's why you got so jealous at the New Year's party then, is it?" He is such a bloody liar!

"I wasn't jealous, I, I just didn't want you there with him that's all!" He is beginning to falter already and I know I should probably back off, but it's too late now and my mouth is running away with me.

"You are such a fucking liar, Dan!" I yell angrily, causing a couple to turn back and look at us before shaking their heads in pity and walking towards the lift.

"Look…"

"Don't bother – just leave me alone." I swing my bag round and start trying to run away down the hall, not as quickly as I would have liked. Running after me he grabs my arm as I try and fight him off, but he is too strong for me, so I am forced to hear him out.

"Sophie, listen to me, I like you, you know that, but it's complicated."

"So uncomplicate it," I say sulkily.

"I can't, I'm with Chloe and I love her – I just, well, I do like you…"

"I know, you've told me before, you're confused."

He nods. It appears I don't even deserve an answer or a real explanation, just a nod. He infuriates me so much and once again, before I can stop myself, my mouth is open and a string of words are pouring out of it.

"You know you'd better make up your mind, Dan – you can't string me along forever." Wow! Considering that was me talking and it was unplanned that was pretty articulate and even sounded quite grown-up. I must have picked it up from a film somewhere. He looks at me and for a second I think he is actually going to give me a proper answer or a decision, but then he just lets go of my arm and we spend the rest of the journey to the airport and home in silence, which was really hard work for me. I had to amuse myself doing work and talking to an old lady who was sitting next to me on the plane.

When he drops me off at home, instead of going straight upstairs I head for my car and decide that a drive is the best idea to clear my head and sort myself out a bit. I wouldn't usually tell Emily, at least not until the drink was flowing, but I had already phoned her detailing how amazing Dan was being, and it was going to be so embarrassing having to tell her that, once again, I was wrong. It will be even worse as well, as she has sorted stuff out with Sam and is all loved up again, which is great for her but sucks for me. I think she just gets bored of having to be really tidy all the time at Sam's, as his house is the cleanest thing I have been in – Kim and Aggy would be proud!

* * *

After about half an hour of mindless driving I find myself driving by Brantano shoe shop for the third time and so decide to have a quick peek. Late night opening really was made for people like me, and an hour later accidentally leave with four new pairs of shoes. The thing is, though, they had a sale on and I needed cheering up, and I had to get them in all the colours they had. Plus, I did just buy this new outfit and needed a pair of pale blue stilettos to go with it…

178

"Where have you been?" says Emily, rushing out into the hallway as I eventually make my way back into the flat. "I thought your flight got in three hours ago, and what is all that?" she says, spotting the bags in my hands.

"I need a drink," is all I say, as I realise that I can't possibly tell her without some vodka in my system.

"Okay," she replies, looking slightly wary as she heads straight for the kitchen and pulls a bottle of vodka and a carton of orange juice out of the fridge.

"Thanks," I say, as I sink down onto the sofa, still clutching my shopping bags in my hands.

After bringing out my drink and watching me down it in one, Emily listens open-mouthed as I tell her the whole horrific story, tears seeping from my eyes as I finish.

"Oh, sweetheart, come here," she says, throwing herself on me and nearly suffocating me with her boobs as she hugs me tightly.

"Sorry," I say weakly, "I just really thought that my dreams were coming true, in terms of Dan and me anyway." I sniff pathetically as I say this and reach for my third vodka, which is sitting half empty on the coffee table.

"He's a twat, Soph, didn't I say you were better off going for James?"

"Yes but he ran away, all the way to LA!"

"Look, we will sort this all out! Besides, you never know, maybe this is the push Dan needed to end things with Chloe, if that's what you both really want."

I don't even know what I want anymore. More vodka, that's what I want, and a knight in shining armour, or maybe I'll just

179

go and live on a little island with my tortoises somewhere nice and hot and I can live off coconuts and bananas…

"So let's have a look at your 'cheer yourself up' shoes then."

"Here." I pass her the bags, not even getting up the energy to be excited by my new shoes, which is very unlike me. It's not right how men can just completely upset the balance of life and change even the way we feel about something as important as shoes when they are being bastards.

"These are gorgeous," she exclaims, pulling out the leopard-print wedges I bought in case we go anywhere with a beach, which to be honest is a long time coming. I mean, I love going to all the cities, so many shops etc. and the sights are amazing, but I haven't been sent anywhere really hot and exotic in a long time.

"Oh my word." She has just pulled out the blue ones, and despite myself I get a little excited as I see the same twinkle in her eyes as I'm sure was in mine when I first saw them.

"They're stunning, aren't they?" I say, smiling for the first time since I got home.

"Hey, they would match that new dress you bought the other day," she exclaims.

"I know," I say, throwing my legs round so I am facing her on the sofa, nearly spilling my drink everywhere as I do so.

"If only we could marry shoes," Emily sighs. "They would never let us down, and when they get worn out we can just get them re-soled."

"I'm sure there must be somewhere in America where you can," I giggle, as we stare almost lustfully at the shoes for a second, and two hours later, with the bottle of vodka empty, we are giggling uncontrollably and I am performing a mock wedding ceremony between Emily and my new orange lace-up stilettos.

Chapter Nineteen
Talking things over

Okay, so I haven't really spoken to Dan since Paris two weeks ago. Luckily, I haven't really had to see him either, because I was up in Liverpool doing some research for another project and then I worked from home this week. So now I am a bit nervous about spending three days in Vienna with him. Not being able to settle, I am pottering around the flat, picking things up aimlessly and putting them down again. Walking to the window, I watch the heavy rain creating torrents of water across the pavement below, hitting the cars so hard that I can hear it. It reminds me of the time Dan and I were stranded in the middle of nowhere in Poland and we just stood there laughing as we watched the rain wash away all the soil underneath our feet. Great! Now I am thinking about him again and I need a distraction. I need to talk this whole thing through before it drives me crazy. Picking up my phone, I flick through my contacts list until I reach Kate's number. We had said that we should catch up soon and go for a coffee, so dialling her number I hold the phone to my ear almost nervously.

"Hello?"

"Hey, Kate, it's me," I say.

"Oh hey, Sophie, you alright?"

"Yeah I'm fine. I was just wondering, are you busy?" I ask, still staring out of the window as I wait for her response.

"No, not really, I was just pottering around and doing some marking."

Marking! Kate, the teacher! It still strikes me as odd when my friends who are teachers talk about 'teacher stuff' like marking. It's just that, in my head, I still feel like it was only a couple of years ago when we, well okay I, hated teachers.

"Good, then you can come round mine for a drink?" I say, not giving her a chance to say no.

"Okay then."

"I'll see you in twenty minutes then." And with that, I hang up the phone and run to the kitchen, rooting around in the back of the cupboard for a couple of bottles of wine and some crisps and peanuts – I forgot I had those... oh well, might as well put them in a bowl. Then, heading back into the living room, I pick out a couple of 'chick flick' DVDs that we can play in the background while she helps solve my problems, and then I sit and twiddle my thumbs while I wait for her to get here. Thinking about it, my life feels a bit like a movie at the moment. I mean, there I was, a normal ordinary girl with a shoe fetish and very bad taste in men. Okay, not completely normal, but if you take out the married man, the travelling, the abnormal amount of spending and the lots of drinking then I was pretty normal. Even the whole 'being in love with my work partner' isn't unheard of, is it? But then it all had to get weird, and he just had to know a movie director who was more perfect than anything I have ever seen and who decided he liked me too. Then, in typical fashion, I made the wrong decision and turned him away so that he ran away back to America and I haven't heard a peep out of him since! But then everything looked up because Dan said he liked me, and then in Paris I thought we were together but that was all a fake, and now I have to go to Vienna with him. ARGH! I hate men, they're just so bloody complicated.

"So what's wrong?" says Kate matter-of-factly, as she sits down with a large glass of wine and a handful of peanuts.

"Oh nothing."

Why do I always say that when I have clearly just told her there is something wrong and that is the reason for her being here?

"Okay, so what's not wrong?"

"Well, it's just that I don't know what to do about the whole situation with Dan."

"What situation? I thought you just admired him from afar?"

"I did, but it's got way out of control now," I sigh.

"Really? Tell me all," her eyes alive with interest as she sits up, trying to get the information out of me by staring at me as hard as she can.

Starting from the beginning I proceed to tell her the whole woeful tale. When I am finally finished, I wait with baited breath for her to solve all my problems and tell me what I need to do.

"What a bastard!"

"Kate!" I say, almost laughing at the sudden outburst from this usually very polite girl.

"Well he is! I wouldn't bother, Sophie, you can do so much better than that."

"But I really like him, I mean really like him, and I just don't know if I can forget about it all and move on."

"What about James?"

"Have you been speaking to Emily?" I ask suspiciously.

"No, why?" she asks, looking back at me.

"Because that's exactly what she asked me," I reply, thinking conspiracy straight away. I have a very cynical mind sometimes, which isn't improved by the way I feel that the world is against me at the moment.

"See!" she yells excitedly.

"See what?"

"It's fate, you and James are the ones who are supposed to be together, not you and Dan, and that's why everything has gone wrong for you because it's a sign."

You have to be joking! Fate? She's crazy – I always said it was a mistake to go back into school once you have left it... teaching clearly turns your brain to mush.

"A big drawback could be that James is in America and I haven't heard anything from him in nearly two months now!" I say, slumping back into the seat and feeling the hurt of rejection all over again.

"But that's because you have to tell him to come back. You need to phone him or something, get in contact."

"I have."

"What?"

Okay, I wasn't actually planning on telling anyone that, it just kind of slipped out – oops.

"I wrote to him and he never replied," I say, wincing slightly as I think about it.

"When? Maybe he hasn't had a chance to yet," she says, looking optimistic.

"A week after he left."

"Oh."

"Exactly. Oh," I repeat dejectedly, as we both spend a few minutes in silence pondering the facts and deciding what the next step should be.

"Dan isn't all bad," I say after a few minutes.

"He isn't?" Kate replies sceptically, clearly not exactly believing me.

"No. I mean he's confused. I know he likes me – he tells me he likes me – and he did send me a rose on Valentine's Day."

"Well yeah, but he also led you on and sent you very mixed signals."

"Oh, I don't know what to do," I cry out in frustration.

"I don't know why you're complaining really."

"What?" I'm astounded she doesn't fully empathise with my woe!

"Think about it, your dilemma is that you have problems with two blokes. Granted, one is a bit of a dick, but still, he is good looking and has all the same interests as you – travel and writing – and the other one is a gorgeous film director who lives in Hollywood and is a perfect gentleman."

"Okay, but…"

"But nothing. My advice to you is have fun. Play Dan at his own game but don't forget that James is still there, and if he comes back or if he contacts you then jump at the chance and go with him."

"Problem solved," I laugh. "Time for a film, I think."

"You know, I think I should be a love guru or something," she muses, as I put 'What a Girl Wants' on and pour out some more wine.

I don't think I'll tell her that she hasn't quite solved all my problems and I still don't exactly know how to speak to Dan when I see him (will the embarrassment ever fade!), but still, at least I can now see that maybe life isn't quite as bad as I thought it was, and hey, at least neither of these two are married! I smile to myself as we settle down to watch the film.

Chapter Twenty
Kiss and Make Up

Bit weird, but I seem to be acting like nothing has happened between us. We met up yesterday to talk over the plans and I was actually sick in the morning before we met I was so nervous and embarrassed, but when we got there he was the same old Dan and it was just like nothing had ever happened. We chatted and laughed and talked over plans, and Paris was never mentioned, not once. To be honest, I don't know whether that's a good thing or not, but I just kept thinking about what Katie had said and decided to just go with it but make sure I was in control this time.

Now we are sitting in the airport waiting for our flight, Dan is reading a book and I am flicking through my new copy of Vogue.

"Hello."

"Hi." Okay… strange man talking to me.

"You travel into Italy?"

"Oh, no, Austria."

"It's shame, Italy is beautiful country," he beams as he tells me.

"Oh yes, I know."

"You've been before?"

Of course I bloody have, honestly. Oh actually, maybe I didn't mention that. Oops, that was a bit mean and now I feel kind of sorry for him, and I would give him a hug to apologise but I'm pretty sure that smell that has just nearly made me gag is coming from him. Plus he is starting to scare me just a little with his staring at my boobs.

"Yes, a few times, do you live there?"

"Yes, in Naples."

"That's, err, nice. Your English is very good."

"Thank you, but it is still not so good."

Well it is, otherwise I wouldn't have said it, would I? Bloody men, fishing for a compliment, that's what I think. Maybe I should start talking to him in his language.

"Bonjour." Shit, no that's French, isn't it? "Hola, donde esta el banio." I have no idea what that means but the man is looking at me like I am completely deranged and Dan is staring at me open-mouthed.

"What?" I ask, slightly affronted. At least I'm making an effort.

"That's a very poor attempt at Spanish," says Dan.

"So?" I say, still not really understanding what he is saying exactly.

"He's Italian."

"I know, but it's all the same, isn't it?"

Honestly, anyone would think I was talking to him in Japanese or something.

"No, it's not, they're completely different languages," he laughs before turning round and saying something to the man in Italian, making me look really stupid, and I shoot him a look to show him exactly how I feel.

"Sorry," I say to the man sheepishly, and he carries on chatting to me, only I don't have a clue what he is saying and he is starting to ever so slightly creep me out. I am doing my best to keep smiling while subtly kicking Dan to get him to make the man go away, but he isn't paying any attention at all. Eventually, I manage to get rid of him by announcing a trip to the loo, although it took me ten minutes to explain exactly what I meant!

* * *

Sitting in the hotel room that night with my back to Dan's bed, I suddenly feel a lot more awkward. I can hear him on the phone outside in the corridor but I can't make out what he is saying. Getting changed, I sit down in the same position as before, staring out of the window. A few minutes later I hear the door shut as he walks in behind me, but I don't bother to turn round. I wouldn't know what to say if I did. I suddenly wish that it was all as simple as it had sounded when I was drinking wine in my sitting room with Kate or when I was buying shoes. After ten more minutes of complete silence, Dan walks round to my bed and sits next to me, also staring out of the window. This silence is killing me. I hate it, I've never liked it, that's why I always talk so much rubbish, just to fill up all the awkward pauses.

"I'm sorry."

Okay, so that was out of the blue. He could give me some bloody warning or something, instead of just springing the big 'I'm sorry' on me out of nowhere.

"Okay." What else does he expect me to say?

"I treated you like shit and I don't expect you to forgive me, I just wanted to say I was sorry."

"I know."

Oh God, stay in control, Sophie, stay in control.

"I wanted you to know that things have, well, they're pretty much over with me and Chloe."

Oh great, I've officially lost control of this conversation, now what do I do? I can feel my whole body wanting to turn to him and kiss him, but I can't.

"I… I'm sorry," I say. What a twat – couldn't I think of anything better to say than that? Because it's a lie for a start, I'm not sorry at all and he knows I'm not.

"Sophie, please look at me."

He sounds so desperate I can't help but turn to look at him, and looking into his eyes I feel exactly the same as I always did, and I mean, the whole Paris thing was my fault, wasn't it? He didn't mean to lead me on. And I really want things to, at the very least, go back to the way they were. This whole not talking thing isn't changing the way I feel about him and it isn't moving my plans along either.

"I didn't mean to overreact in Paris."

"You didn't, I was a knob."

"Yes I did. If I had done my work and communicated with you more, like you are always telling me to do, then it would never have happened."

"Well, I'm glad it did."

What the bloody hell is he talking about now?

"What?"

"If it hadn't then I wouldn't have known how you felt about me."

"Yeah, because it's really changed things!"

I can't look at him any longer and stare rather intently at the floor in the corner of the room.

"It has actually. That's why I told Chloe I liked you..."

I don't really register what he has just said because I have just seen the hugest spider ever crawl out from underneath the wardrobe. Screaming, I fly up onto the bed leaving him in shocked silence, until he sees me gesturing at the corner of the room where he sees the big furry beast and promptly goes and picks it up and throws it out of the window. Coming back towards me he grabs my hand and pulls me down so that I am sitting cross-legged on the bed, still shaking. I really, really, really hate spiders, even more than fish, and they really terrify me!

"I can't believe that after all the travelling we've done you're still scared of spiders," he laughs at me and sits down on the bed opposite, also cross-legged so that our knees are touching.

"I know, but they are just so erghhh," I shudder at the thought of them.

"What would you do without me?" he smiles, holding my

hand.

Oh God, we are about to kiss, I know it, and I should stop it but I don't really want to.

"I... I don't know," I stutter, starting to shake again as he begins to lean a little closer.

Reaching up, he grabs my chin gently with his hand, pulling my face towards his as our lips brush against each other. Well there's no going back now, is there? And whilst I'm pretty sure that this isn't exactly the 'playing him at his own game' Kate was talking about, I'll take it, because after all I have been waiting for over a year to do this. And it really was worth the wait!

Chapter Twenty One
Birthdays and Boyfriends

I am so excited I am literally bouncing off the walls. I haven't been on a big night out with my girls in months, at least not with all of us together. There's always something getting in the way, usually men! But tonight is my birthday, although that does, of course, mean me becoming another year older. How old am I this year? Bloody hell, I think it might be my twenty-fifth. That's only five years off thirty! I can't be. What year was I born? Eighty-four, so that means... and it's two thousand and eight, so that means... I'm turning... where's the bloody calculator on this phone? Oh twenty-four! That's not quite as bad, but I will definitely be using my birthday money to stock up on my anti-wrinkle creams, that is after I've paid off the bills for my gorgeous New Year's dress of course. I can drink away my worries of getting old tonight and I get to do it with all the girls. No boyfriends, no fiancés or husbands, and no exceptions, except Alex of course, but he doesn't count. Not because he's gay or anything, which he is, but that doesn't have anything to do with it because I think even if he wasn't he would still be practically one of the girls anyway. Oh and definitely no designated drivers.

What's that noise? I don't remember turning the radio on. Oh shit it's my phone again. Why does it always go off just when I've put it away? Now where did I put it? Rummaging around my desk I eventually find it in the drawer, though how it ended up in there I will never know, and flipping it open I put it to my ear.

"Hello."

"Happy Birthday to you, Happy Birthday to you, Happy Birthday my little baby, Happy Birthday to youuuuuuu."

"Hi, Mum," I laugh, as she draws breath after the final note.

"Sweetheart, I can't believe it, twenty-four."

"Alright, rub it in!" I exclaim. She nearly killed me when I sent balloons with happy fiftieth written on them to work for her birthday.

"So..."

"So?" I question. What is she talking about now?

"Are you looking forward to your night out?" Anyone would think I was going out for the first time the way she is speaking.

"Yes Mum, it should be a laugh, why don't you come along for a few drinks?"

"Oh darling, you don't want me there cramping your style."

"Well number one, no one can cramp my style," – it's true, my style is so good it's truly uncrampable, well I think so anyway, some may disagree – "and two, I wouldn't have asked you if I didn't want you to come, would I?"

"I would love to, sweetie, but your father and I are going out to that school charity concert tonight."

"Oh yeah, I forgot about that."

"Well have fun tonight, don't get too drunk will you, and Happy Birthday."

"Thanks, Mum, have a good night at your ball thing."

"Bye, sweetie, love you."

"Bye." Putting down the phone I smile to myself, for a moment thinking about all the mental birthday parties my mum had arranged for me over the years. Mind you, this will be one of the most hectic, messy, mental birthdays yet.

I bought my birthday outfit nearly a month ago and it has been sitting in my wardrobe next to my outfit for 'GMTV' ever since, and I admire it every time I open the doors. I really do have very good taste. Right okay, so I chose a black and pink theme for the outing, and the only other rule is to look as glamorous as possible and wear high heels! Not that this rule went down too well with everyone; I don't think Ruth was too happy about wearing heels and I'm pretty sure that there are a couple who aren't exactly keen about the pink, but there you go, my party, my rules! The shoes I have bought are amazing! Okay so granted, I already have the same ones in black and silver, and maybe in red too (but those ones are hidden and not to be mentioned until after my birthday when I can pretend they were a present), but these ones are hot pink, round-toed, in a suede-like material, with a wooden stacked heel and a pink ribbon that wraps around the ankle and ties off. I LOVE THEM! To be honest, I could probably go out completely naked and it wouldn't matter, because they are so amazing that nobody will be looking at anything other than the shoes. But I did buy the rest of the outfit just in case I get arrested for indecent exposure or something, although that might be fun. I bought a black pencil skirt and a hot pink shirt to tuck into it and I have to say, that teamed with a black cardigan, I look sophisticated and still hot. I have to admit that the outfit's sophistication is slightly let down by the huge flashing birthday badge that practically covers my whole left boob, but Emily insists I have to wear it along with the balloons that I am informed will be tied to my wrist.

* * *

Time to go to the hairdressers. A rule I have is that I am not allowed to go to any big events, meaning weddings or massive nights out, or my own birthdays, without having my hair done and my nails airbrushed with a new pattern to match the outfit that I will be wearing that night.

Entering the hairdressers, I greet Joel warmly. I love him – best hairdresser I could ask for and a great drinking buddy, too. He's Australian and we always chat about the relatives I have out there and then we get onto the subject of beer and surfing, at which point I tend to daydream about him half-naked in the sea while he massages my head and practically sends me to sleep. After my usual two hours of pampering and with amazing new shiny, beautiful hair, I head straight for the nail shop to get them filled in and a new pattern applied. After much deliberation, I finally settle on a hot pink and gold flower pattern, which I admire along with my hair all the way home – come to think about it they should really take interior mirrors out of cars as they just cause problems. I nearly crashed at least three times on the way home whilst admiring either my hair or my nails…

* * *

At seven o'clock, as I am applying the final touches to my make-up with a very shaky hand (probably not a good idea to drink a bottle of wine before putting on the mascara, but there you go, I blame Emily for buying it!), a knock on the front door distracts me and, once again, I end up with a big blob of black on my nose. Bugger, although I can't help laughing. I've been doing that a lot in the last half hour, but this time it is genuinely funnier than the other five times I've done it because I look even more like a panda than I did before.

"Sophie?"

That would be Carly here then.

"Oi! Sophie, get your arse out here and have a drink."

Okay, Tanya has entered the building and I'm pretty sure this is where my night is going to start getting messy. Wiping off the black smudge I take a deep breath, try to steady myself and then teeter out into the hallway to join the growing group of girls there.

"Where's Emily?" I ask, looking around as I hug Tanya and Carly, who are standing in the hallway.

"She's gone to get Alex," comes a voice from the kitchen.

"Ruth! I didn't realise you were here!" I beam, moving through to find her and a work surface full of bottles.

"Couldn't miss this," she squeals, hugging me tightly.

"So, how's married life treating you then?"

"Oh, it's okay."

"Okay?" I ask, giving her my most sober, concerned expression, or at least what I think is a sober expression, but I can feel my eyes wandering a little to the open bottle of champagne bubbling over into the sink.

"Yeah, it's pretty much the same as before to be honest, except I do love being able to say hello, I'm Mrs Willcocks..." she blushes and takes a huge gulp of her drink as she says this.

"Bloody hell, Mrs Willcocks, I never even thought of you as a Mrs. That's really scary, like a proper grown-up."

I stand still, well with a slight sway, and contemplate the fact that my friends are actually becoming real world people and doing grown-up things like buying houses and getting married.

"Stop moping and get this down you," Alex booms, as he walks in carrying a bottle of Sambucca in his hand, and looking as camp and gorgeous as ever.

"Hey babe!" I scream, jumping on him as he squeezes me to the point where I think I might explode, considering I am currently about ninety-nine percent alcohol. As we break apart I see Emily struggling in behind him carrying the biggest box I have ever seen.

"What's that?" I ask, my interest immediately aroused.

"That would be your birthday present from Alex and me," says Emily, panting as she tries to catch her breath and grabbing a glass off Carly, downing it in one and promptly filling it up again, obviously trying to catch up with the rest of us as quickly as possible.

"What is it?" I squeak excitedly.

"Open it, you twat," Alex grins, sitting on the arm of the chair and taking a swig of Sambucca straight from the bottle.

"Okay," I mutter almost nervously, stepping towards the huge parcel and grabbing the massive pink bow that is sitting on top of it.

Opening it, I am confronted with tons of shredded coloured paper with various wrapped-up presents poking out. Wow, I love these sorts of presents, they're amazing. I can feel my smile spreading across my face to the extent that it feels like it will split. Diving my arms in, I pull out the first present and, unwrapping it, find a beautiful black and silver corset top.

"It's stunning!" I gasp, holding it up to me and already considering changing, but realising that I would have to rethink the whole outfit if I were to do that and I may already be too drunk to think that through properly.

"Open the rest of them," cry out the group gathered around me.

"Okay, give me a chance," I say, slopping a little champers onto the carpet and hoping that Emily doesn't notice.

* * *

Forty minutes later, I have finished opening all my presents, which are all safely back in the box so that I don't ruin them and can actually look at them and remember what they are without forgetting five minutes later. We have all managed to finish about six bottles and are stumbling down the stairs towards the two cabs that are waiting for us at the bottom. Sitting in the cab, I can feel my head spinning very quickly as I try to make it stop by closing my eyes, and opening them quickly when I realise that this only has the effect of making me feel as if I am on a high-speed upside-down spinning-round rollercoaster. Fuck, I think I'm going to be sick. Hold it in, hold it in, oh yuck, I just swallowed a little bit of sick! Never mind, we're nearly there, and as we pull up I jump out and find a bush to be sick in. There is a group of blokes walking past and they shout something out, but I don't even try and hear what they are saying as I finish being sick and pull out my toothbrush. I know, a toothbrush in my bag for a night out, some might think I am being a bit presumptuous and expecting to go home with someone, but I promise you that is not it at all. It is there for these precise occasions!

Now, I have a little travel tube of toothpaste somewhere in here… oh bugger! That's everything all over the place! Spinning round to pick them up, I find myself sitting on the floor surrounded by the contents of my handbag. Emily and Carly are laughing so hard they can barely move or breathe, and Tanya seems to be imitating me until I realise that she has just fallen up a kerb by accident and is spreadeagled on the floor herself. Looking up, I see Alex giving us all a look of mock disapproval before handing me my toothpaste and picking up my stuff while I brush my teeth and get ready to carry on for the night.

"Right," I slur, attempting to stand up and pull down my skirt.

"On to the club!" yell Kate and Carly in unison, pointing and then marching forwards for a couple of metres before collapsing in another fit of giggles.

* * *

201

After spending the next three hours dancing and singing and drinking lots and lots and lots of shots, I decide that it's time for me to go home. So wandering, okay staggering, out of the club, I reach for my phone and somehow, without my brain consenting to it, my hands are dialling Dan's number.

"Hello," his voice sounds gravelly and sexy, but I am pretty sure I just woke him up.

"Hey," I say lightly, giggling as I dodge a kebab that has been dropped all over the floor and nearly fall over again.

"Sophie, what are you doing! It's two in the morning."

"I was just out for my birthday, cos it's my birthday," I slur.

"Okay…"

"So, what are you doing?" I ask in my sexiest drunk voice.

"Sleeping," he replies shortly. Oops, now this is the point where I should just say goodbye, but for some reason my fuzzy brain won't tell my hands to hang up the phone and my mouth just keeps saying things.

"Anyway, I was just thinking I haven't seen you since like last week," I begin, pausing to figure out exactly where this is going, when I trip up a curb in front of two blokes who start jeering at me as I scream and drop my phone. Bollocks, I cut him off. Oh well! Standing up again I start to make my way to where I am pretty sure the kebab men wait, I mean the… no, what do I mean? Oh brain, why aren't you working! Cab men, that's the one.

"And do you know, do you knoooow," I begin to sing aloud. I wonder how that song got into my head, and my arm is vibrating. That tickles, oh that would be my phone! After a few attempts, as my fingers seem to have suddenly either turned into large sausages or fused together, I manage to pull it out of my bag and flip it open.

"Hello."

"Sophie, babe, are you alright?" Dan sounds panicky about something, I wonder what he's done.

"Yes, I'm fine," I reply.

"Why didn't you answer your phone? I've just phoned you about eight times!"

"Why?" He is odd. Why would he phone me so many times?

"Because I heard you scream and these men yelling and I thought something had happened!"

"Oh, you do care…" I say before I can stop myself.

"Of course I care, I thought you would have got that when I kissed you in Vienna." He makes a good point.

"I suppose."

"So are you okay? What are you doing now?"

"I'm going to get the kebab man to drive me home."

"The what?"

"The cab driver man?" I repeat. Honestly, anyone would think he was the drunk one. "But actually, I don't have any money, so maybe I'll find someone to share with me, oh EXCUSE ME," I yell to a couple of girls who are wandering past and just look at me as if I'm deranged. "Rude," I say, quite affronted by their silence towards me.

"Where are you?"

"In town."

"Right. Go and stand by the post office and I will be there in ten minutes," he says, and I can hear him rushing around and

203

pulling things about as I stand at the end of the phone.

"But…"

"Just go stand there, Sophie, okay?"

Hanging up the phone I'm not quite sure what to think. I feel suddenly a lot more sober and rush to the post office, where I sit down and discover a few ladders in my tights – well actually they're ripped to pieces and both my knees are quite badly bleeding, but I am not quite sober enough to feel it, thank God!

Seeing his car screech up and him jump out, I am suddenly so overcome with want for him that I really just want to jump on him, but luckily the alcohol has seeped out of me enough that I manage to control myself. Running over to me he looks totally shocked, which to be fair can be excused by the fact that I look a little like I have been in a fight: my legs are bruised and bleeding, my shirt is ripped, and catching a glimpse of myself in the window as he helps me up I see that my make-up is all over the place. Getting into the car he puts my seatbelt on for me and then, getting back into the driver's seat, kisses me lightly before starting the car.

Pulling up outside my building I look up at him and decide that this is definitely my chance to get together once and for all.

"So are you coming up?" I ask quietly.

"Well I can't leave you to struggle up the stairs on your own, can I?" he replies coyly, as he parks and hurries round to help me out of the car, my shoes now in my hands as I could no longer suffer in them. Together we walk hand-in-hand up to the flat, where I hand him the key. Dropping everything in the hallway

I stretch my arms up round his neck as he kisses me, pushing my back against the front door making it click shut. Making our way down the hall I can feel his hands all over my body, as first my shirt then my skirt drop to the floor. As I pull his shirt off I start kissing his chest as my hands try and undo the belt he is wearing. All of a sudden, however, as I am once again pinned against the wall, James pops into my head and I can't shift the memory of kissing him here in this same place only a couple of months ago. Moving into my bedroom, which as I recall is further than I ever went with James, he pushes me onto the bed and climbs on top of me, kissing my neck, making my back arch with his touch, and for some reason I seem to forget James's face for the moment.

Chapter Twenty Two
A weekend away

I can do this, I mean, so what if it's only the Peak District and not the Caribbean? I've heard it's a very pretty place, plus they drink a lot up there apparently, so there will at least be loads of pubs around. Besides, Dan's not with Chloe any more so this is like our first holiday together, and if it's going to be anything like the other night it will definitely be a weekend to remember.

I don't think I've stopped thinking about that night for a second, not that I remember a huge amount of it to be honest. I remember being in Dan's car, and then in the flat, and for some weird reason James was there for a minute, although I think I may have imagined that bit. Oh and then we were in bed, that bit was good, I think, then I woke up in the morning and Dan left to go… I can't remember where he was going but I remember the pain, bloody hell it was like I'd been boxing, but it was worth it. But now I must focus and put together my suitcase for the weekend. That sounds so grown-up, a weekend away together. Even if we are technically going for work and have in fact been away for weekends hundreds of times with work, this is the first time we've been working 'away'!

Since we kissed and well you know, the whole birthday thing happened, and he told me he had split up with Chloe – okay, so he didn't actually say that he had broken up with her for me, but I know that's what he meant – the clothes I wear are imperative to the success of our future relationship. I have to look (or at least try, probably unsuccessfully, to look) as glamorous and sexy as Chloe, but at the same time remain me and so a little bit quirky. I'll tell you now that it is bloody hard work. I have always maintained, however, that I have a better eye for style than Chloe and definitely a better taste in shoes – God, that woman owned some horrific slabs of fabric that she reported were in fact shoes! I think at the end of the day the shoes could have made all the difference between us, and that this is what has driven him away from her and towards me!

Emily says that in order to win a man's heart, don't do it through his stomach – a good thing, because if that was the case I would be doomed to live out my days as a spinster with hundreds of… not cats, that's a bit cliché, let's try, yes, turtles. But to do it through a good wardrobe, if you always wear the right outfit, you can never go wrong. It gets across your feelings perfectly, and I have to say she's right.

Anyway, focus, so I need a travelling outfit, then an outfit for when we get there, one for dinner that night, then there's the two for Saturday during the day, the outfit choices for Saturday night, and the same for Sunday, and lastly, an outfit for travelling home. So I think if I go with something simple like the plain black peeptoe stilettos I bought last week for the travelling, then I can wear them with skinny jeans and a black camisole with a big red belt to dress it up a little bit – the perfect travelling ensemble. And I think I'll have my hair up in a loose bun with a bit of black eyeliner but mostly natural make-up, it'll be perfect. Sinking down onto the edge of my bed, I daydream about the romantic weekend with Dan, with him picking me up in his open-top car (artistic licence, I mean, I know he doesn't actually have a soft-top car, but in my dreams he always seems to be driving a Porsche and has a few more muscles going on).

"Sophie?" Well that rudely awakened me from my fantasies.

"In here," I call out, as I hear Emily padding down the hallway towards my bedroom door.

"Can I borrow those blue suede shoes?"

"Which ones? The flats or the stilettos?" I reply without looking up from my folding.

"The stilettos."

"Okay, oh, which ones? The kitten heels with the peep-toes or the stacked heels with the rounded toes?" I glance up at her briefly as she picks her way across my floor, which is strewn with discarded suitcase options.

"Erm, the stacked heels I think," she says, as she begins rooting around in the bottom of my wardrobe.

"They're over here in the brightly coloured shoebox under the left side of the bed," I say matter-of-factly, as she grins and trots over towards me, throwing herself down on the bed behind me and leaning down, heaving the box out. I glance back nervously to make sure she has not spotted my secret shoebox.

"So," she says as she sits back, panting after pulling them out of the overloaded Perspex box.

"So," I smile at her over my shoulder.

"You really ready for this trip tomorrow?"

"Why wouldn't I be?" I look at her puzzled.

"I don't know, it's just you've liked him for so long and well, I just… you don't think he might be on the rebound?"

"No! I mean, I know he's just split up with her but it's been rocky for a while now and I know he likes me, he has for a long time." Oh great, she's raising her eyebrows at me. She always does that when she thinks I'm wrong but doesn't want to tell me in case I go off on one.

"Okay," she says not very convincingly as she stands up.

"Where are you off to anyway?" I say, trying to change the subject.

"I'm staying at Sam's for a couple of nights, he wants to sort things out." She sounds reluctant just talking about it.

"Oh," I say in what I think is an understanding voice. They've been having a few rows ever since their relationship status went back to boyfriend/girlfriend.

"Yeah, 'oh' is the right word. In fact, scrap my warnings, it would be better if it was just a fling. Saves all this bloody trouble, trust me, you're better off without men."

"It is not a rebound, okay? Look, you'll see after this weekend, we'll be together properly at last."

"What about James?" she asks suddenly.

"God, I haven't even thought about him since Paris," I say, feeling guilty for some reason.

"Well I thought you were still deciding between the two of them."

"I was, I am, I mean, I don't know. I've always loved Dan, you know that, and James... well, he was perfect and everything, but it would never have really worked, would it? I mean he lives in Hollywood for fuck's sake! And I haven't heard from him in ages!"

"Okay, I get what you mean, as long as you're sure, and be careful." She hugs me and gives me a kiss before running off as if she's about to leave, when I know that she will probably still be getting ready when I leave in the morning. Throwing my suitcase on the floor, I decide the best idea is to get an early night, but three hours later I am still tossing and turning, James popping into my head every few minutes as I try and block him out. Why did Emily have to bring him up and confuse things? Dan's the one I want, he's the one who's here. I mean, I haven't even heard from James since he went back to America over three months ago, not even after I wrote him that letter for Valentine's Day. Getting up I figure that packing will help me sleep and, sure enough, after two more complete repacks and a quick tidy of my room, which now no longer resembles a bombsite, I am absolutely knackered and fall straight to sleep (with a bit of 'One Tree Hill' on in the background).

* * *

Sitting on the edge of the sofa the next morning I feel sick with anticipation, and my suitcase is stuffed full and sitting by the front door along with my vanity case. My handbag is clutched so tightly in my hands that I think I may have damaged the leather, and I'm pretty sure I'll be picking out little bits of the material from underneath my nails for weeks. I'm tapping my feet on the floor and glancing up into the mirror every five seconds, and the TV's on but I can barely concentrate on it. This is ridiculous, I say to myself, I'm acting like I'm going on my first date or something. As my phone rings I jump into the air and nearly fall off my shoes in fright.

"Get a grip," I say aloud to myself. Walking down to the car – I say walking, it's more a case of stumbling – with my suitcase behind me, by the time I get to the car I've already sweated half my make-up off. Bollocks, not the best start. Smiling, he opens the door from the inside and jumps out to help put my stuff in the back. The knots in my stomach are just as tight as ever as I sit almost nervously next to him and we set off. Relaxing slightly as he flicks on a CD, I lean back, staring out of the window, and we remain in silence for most of the journey.

* * *

Pulling up to a cottage four hours later, I gasp in admiration at Dan's choice of the place to stay, completely on its own in the middle of nowhere, really in the middle of nowhere actually. As I look around I can't see anything except fields and mountains; it's even more remote than that place in the South of France we were at last year. Shutting my mouth suddenly, I follow him quickly inside and, grabbing my suitcase, yell at him to put the kettle on while I change. Walking into the only bedroom containing a fourposter bed my heart gives a little leap, and hauling the case onto the bed I unzip it and pull out my brand new pink stilettos and tight black trousers with the pink halter-neck top. These shoes are so gorgeous, he is going to love them.

Walking back out after a quick make-up re-application and brush of my hair, I glance at him as he looks up from his coffee cup and, smiling, stands up and walks over towards me.

"Wow," he says, grabbing for my hand, and I just stand there. I can't speak or anything, I just stand looking at his chest and blushing.

"Erm, so…" I fail completely to say anything audible or that makes any sense.

"I haven't really had a chance to see you much since, well, since your birthday."

"I know, I just thought I'd give you space," I say.

"Why?" he asks bemused.

"Because of you and Chloe," I reply.

"Ah babe, you know me and her have been pretty much over for ages now."

"That's the bit that worries me, the pretty much over." I look up at him, meeting his eyes as he grabs my head in both hands.

"Well we are… pretty much." As he finishes speaking he pulls my head forward and kisses me roughly, his tongue pushing its way into my mouth, and for a moment I let myself get lost in the lust of it, until what he has just said suddenly rushes back into my head and I pull away quickly.

"What do you mean, pretty much?"

"We're on a break."

"What?" My voice is rising already.

"We, well, we're temporarily separated but you know,

we probably won't get back together." Oh you have got to be joking.

I have just been played by my lifetime lust, and I am so angry I'm shaking.

"You told me you had split up."

"We have, sort of," he says, as if he is actually confused.

"Being on a break and being split up are two completely different things," I almost scream.

"But I said I liked you, Soph."

"So, oh God, what about when we kissed in Vienna and you said you had just ended it with her!"

"I did, I mean we had a row," he says, his defences up as he backs off slightly.

"You bastard." Tears are now streaming down my face as I try desperately to stop them, but I can't.

"Babe, come on, don't get upset."

"Upset? Dan, you know what happened with Kevin and you have just gone and done the same thing!" I stutter at him, trying to control my shaking voice.

"No, it's not the same, I never meant…"

"Yeah well you did, didn't you? Wanted the best of both worlds: a quick shag with me to see how it goes and then if you decide you don't want me, it's back home to your perfect girlfriend!"

"No, it's not like that, she's not perfect. I want you, honestly!"

"OH JUST FUCK OFF, DAN!" I scream at him, and I slap him so hard round the face that I think I may have broken my hand. Shit that hurt, a lot. Standing there I watch him hold his face for a second, and then seeing as he doesn't seem to be moving and I really can't stand to be around him at the moment I decide to leave. So stamping on his foot and listening to him cry out in pain, I run as quickly as I can on my heels out of the cottage and off towards the hills behind it.

The first rule of life… never let them see you cry, and I just broke it. I thought he was the one. I thought after everything, all the heartache, all the chasing, so much pain, I thought that at last I'd picked the right one! I waited, I didn't jump in. I sat back, made friends, got close and I tried, oh God I tried so hard not to get pulled into it all again, but I fell, hard! I pushed others away, well okay I didn't have any others really to speak of to push away… but I would have pushed them away if I'd had any, and actually I did! I pushed James away, sort of. He was perfect, too perfect, and I am so used to absolute idiots that I assumed it was all just a game he was playing, but no, he was actually perfect and I let him go all the way to the other side of the world and to all the beautiful stick-thin famous people, all because I chose Dan over him, and look what I got for it… another slap in the face. I giggle a little at the memory of his face with a nice big hand print across it, and then sniff again as I remember why it is that he has a slap mark there. I can't believe I fell for that shit again. I must literally be the most gullible person on the planet, seriously, and what's worse, not only did I just let him see how upset I was – never a good thing when I have to see him at work, because now I can't pretend like it was nothing – but I was the one who left instead of making him walk out, and I think that might have possibly been the most ridiculous thing I have done so far. Okay, correction, this was definitely the most stupid, really, really stupid idea. I really should have made him leave, as it's his fault after all. God, I can't believe I was taken in by his smooth talking. When will I learn that all men are absolute, complete and utter bastards?

Pushing my hair angrily off my forehead, I stop to catch my breath and find out where I am. I'm surrounded by muddy fields and mountains and have absolutely no idea how the hell I got here, and to top it all off my bloody shoes are ruined – they were new as well. I spent a fortune on them to impress Dan, the bastard. Right, no point in pouting, I have to get out of here first, find a pub or something and drink large amounts of vodka. Yeah, that's what I need to do, and then phone Em and get her to come and pick me up. I'll write the article based mostly on my research, it'll be fine.

Oh great, now it's raining as well, brilliant, my make-up is going to run and I didn't put waterproof mascara on today. Pausing for shelter under a tree, I begin to feel a slight panic rising in the pit of my stomach, not unlike the panic that I feel every time I get lost in a foreign country. But this is worse, much worse. Okay so granted, I'm not in a foreign country, just the Peak District, but I'm in the countryside! I mean, whenever I get lost in a city or a town or even a village, anywhere in the world, I'm okay because even if they don't speak any English there's always some form of a bar around. So I'm okay because I just have a drink and then wait for Dan to come and get me. That's the way it's always been, and now I'm standing in a field, my three-inch heels completely immersed in the mud and I have a funny feeling that after that slap, Dan won't be rescuing me anytime soon. The heavens are really starting to open now and

I think that was lightning! I hate thunderstorms! What do they say to do? Is it stay under a tree or run away from the tree? Oh God, oh God, oh God. Run away. That's what I have to do, run away from the tree into an open area. Crap, okay, didn't mean to fall flat on my face while in the process of running. Picking myself gingerly off the saturated ground, I try to rub the mud off my knees, but succeed only in spreading it further over my legs than before.

This day is not exactly going the way I planned, and wandering around in muddy fields in the rain is definitely not how I pictured spending tonight. Okay, so the rain could be quite romantic if he ran after me and declared his love for me, kissing me in the rain, before heading back to a pre-prepared room full of lit candles and rose petals. I close my eyes trying desperately to picture this happening... not working. Okay, let's carry on walking. My feet are bloody killing me, these shoes may look amazing – well they used to anyway – but I think my feet may by this point be bleeding. Having eventually come to the reality that there will be no romantic encounter in the rain with a dashing young man on horseback, I head further up the mountain. It's getting darker and darker and there is still no pub in sight, and by now I'm bloody freezing as well. Why didn't I bring a bloody coat! I have a little black one that would have matched this outfit perfectly. Stumbling up a slippery bit of loose gravel I nearly slip and fall... and bugger, I just broke a nail. Tears prickle in the back of my eyes again as frustration begins to mount in me.

"I need a drink," I yell, hoping someone will come and take me to a pub, but no, my voice just echoes back at me and I suddenly realise that I am now surrounded by mountains and… what the fuck is that? Oh, it's a sheep! I start laughing hysterically as I realise that I was just terrified of a bloody sheep. My foot suddenly falls forward down a hole halfway towards the sheep and, before I know it, my legs are over my head and I'm tumbling down the bloody thing, landing with one leg in the air and the other one definitely not where it should be. As the pain sears through my body and I grip the grass, I scream out, unable to breathe or focus on anything other than the pain in my leg. Shit, shit, oh God, that hurts so much! I think I've snapped it, oh no, that means no heels for like six weeks! Oh no, how am I going to get home? I'm going to die in a bloody field full of sheep poo and worms and stuff. This is horrible. I'm not supposed to die like this. I need to get famous and get a bloke to fall in love with me and get married and everything, not die here after being screwed over by a bloke again. Owwww, my leg! Oh God, my leg hurts so much. Panic is starting to really rise now and I can feel the cold and wet of the ground soaking into my skin.

"HELP!" I scream out.

"Help," I say more quietly, realising that no one's going to come. Tears are once again, with good reason this time, pouring down my grazed cheeks as I lie there, quietly beginning to think over my life as the aching and dull pain from my leg starts to increase. Come on, Sophie, concentrate on something else.

I can't believe that I've been lying here dying for like four hours! The sun is now coming up and no one has come to save me yet. I really am beginning to give up now and I haven't even written a will… Oh I hope Emily takes my shoes. I couldn't bear for them to be thrown away or given away to people who don't appreciate them.

Chapter Twenty Three
The Perfect Shoes

"Put her in F," a hassled-looking nurse says as I lie on my bed, the morphine by now happily flowing through me.

"No, F's needed for re-suss," my nurse replies.

"No, that's I."

"I is for the diabetic."

"No, that's definitely K," says the increasingly distracted nurse consulting the notes.

"I think K is for the lacerated arm," my nurse is now saying.

"No, that's H."

"No, H is…"

I've now drifted into a new conversation about hats coming from the two old ladies next to me. Oh God, just wheel me into a bloody room already! Or better still, pull a curtain around me here, it will do the same trick!

Eventually, after about ten minutes of arguing over the uses of the various cubicles, they wheel me into one and leave me there, ignoring my request for more morphine. James is sitting beside me and there is an awkward silence as we wait for Emily to park her car and phone the necessary list of people, meaning her entire phonebook. Looking down at my ankle I start to giggle, although perhaps this is largely due to the shock and the morphine, but God it's disgusting. It is actually nearly three times the size of the other one. I'm not going to be able to wear my heels for ages and, oh God, I'd almost briefly forgotten about my wrecked shoes. I can feel my eyes fill with tears as I think about them.

"Are you alright?" James says looking worried, as a small tear escapes my eye without my consent.

"Oh yeah," I say sheepishly, "I was just, it hurts a bit that's all."

"I'll go get a nurse," he says jumping up.

"No, it's fine," I can feel myself blushing slightly as I grab at his arm and try to make him sit back down, just as Emily comes trotting through the curtains looking very happy with herself.

"What are you so happy about?" I ask suspiciously.

"Oh nothing, I just met a really nice person in the car park that's all," she replies coyly.

"By person, do you mean a man?"

"Well yes, but he was in uniform."

"And what about Sam?" Look at me being all responsible. Maybe that knock on the head did something.

"I know, but I can still look, can't I? And he was in uniform, no woman can say no to that."

"I guess not. Was he really hot? Paramedic or fireman?" Okay, maybe that's a no to the bump on the head theory, just a momentary lapse of my normal self I guess.

"Paramedic. Hey listen, I'm just going to get some coffee but I'll be back in a minute, okay?" she says as she swings round, very narrowly missing my leg with her bag as she does so, and then she's gone. Great, now there's nothing for it, I have to speak to him and so I turn to look at him.

"So why are you here?" I hear myself saying. Bloody hell, maybe I did hit my head harder than I thought… why am I being so blunt?

"I came to see you," he says, staring at me and making me shake all over again, and he quickly jumps up and pulls my little silver blanket around me.

"Why?" I stutter.

"Well I've been trying to tell you for so long… you know I like you." What did he just say? The bloody cheek! Men! Honestly.

"Oh. Hang on a minute, how exactly have you been trying to tell me that you like me? By belittling my career, kissing me and then running off back to America and not replying to my letter?" I say, starting to get worked up again.

"I thought the rose would have been a clue."

"What rose?" Honestly, anyone would think that he was the one with a bump on the head, or maybe he just needs me to give him one so he will stop confusing me and just tell me what the bloody hell is going on here.

"The rose I sent on Valentine's Day, with the note saying in preparation for your trip and I wish I could be with you." He

221

looks almost hurt.

"That was you?" I say astounded, trying to sit up. I wince and quickly give up. "That absolute bastard!"

"Who?"

"But you didn't even know I was going away, you had already gone back to Hollywood." Okay, that sounded a little more bitter than I would have liked.

"You told me you were going."

"No I didn't." How dare he smile at me like that? I clearly would remember if I had told him... oh yeah, the party... I may have gloated about my upcoming trips. Shit, how do I get out of this one?

"Yes you did, in the car on the way to the New Year's party." He is so persistent, and I can't let him see that I am wrong again.

"That absolute bastard," I growl, trying to throw him off the conversation.

"Who?"

Success! I am brilliant, even when traumatised and nearly dead.

"Who do you think? Dan! God, I'm going to kill him."

"How about just getting better first." His voice is so bloody soothing he's calming me down... against my will.

"But he stole... well he stole the fact that the rose was from you."

"I think I'll get over it, Sophie. Besides, we'll have plenty of time to think up a suitable punishment."

"Well okay then, but in the meantime I want at least a dozen of those roses."

"Right away, ma'am, they will be at your bedside within the hour."

Giggling, I lean back and close my eyes. I think maybe I picked the wrong bloke; maybe I'll stick with this one for a while.

"Sophie?"

Opening my eyes I nearly have a heart attack as I see a bedraggled-looking Dan standing in front of me.

"What are you doing here?" I ask angrily.

"Sophie, I'm so sorry."

"Go away, Dan."

"Please, Sophie." He steps towards me, reaching out and hitting my leg, causing me to wince in pain and James to stand up.

"Mate, you heard what she said."

"Shut up, James. You wouldn't even be here if I hadn't called."

"What?" Now I'm confused.

"When you ran off and the storm started I went to look for you, and when I couldn't find you I called for help and I called Emily to see if you had made it home, and he was with her. I've been sick with worry."

This is unbelievable.

"What were you doing with Emily?" I exclaim, trying to get at least one answer today.

"I came back to see you," he replies simply.

"Oh," I say, completely shocked.

"Look, Dan, just leave," says James, standing rigidly next to me.

223

"Who are you to tell me to leave? This has nothing to do with you," Dan growls angrily, stepping forward.

"Do you not think you've hurt her enough already?" James takes a step forward too and I can almost smell the testosterone flowing around the cubicle.

"Unlike you of course, 'Mr Perfect', you just show off for a night or two and lead her on before fucking off back to Hollywood!"

"Both of you, shut up," I say rather timidly, trying to assert my authority over them and failing miserably, which I don't mind too much seeing as I have never had two men fighting over me before and I'm quite enjoying it.

"Yeah, because you've been such a solid support to her, haven't you?" James sneers.

Support? What am I, a bloody bench or something?

"At least I'm there, I've always been there!" Dan shouts.

"Oh give me a break, you can hardly call trying to screw around with her while your girlfriend's off in Aspen or wherever, being there for her," laughs James loudly.

Okay, time to stop this, it's starting to get out of control and I don't really want the whole A and E department to hear about my rather tragic sex life.

"Stop it!" I yell, sitting up and trying to separate the two of them before they start throwing punches, but completely misjudging the width of the bed – I mean really, they must have put me on a kid's bed or something because this is just ridiculous, I mean, I know I'm not exactly skinny but come on – I fall straight off the edge of it and go crashing to the floor. Screaming out in pain and slight humiliation, the two men immediately turn their attention to me. Well at least they've stopped fighting for five seconds.

"Leave her, I'll get her up," Dan says irritated, trying to scoop me up off the floor.

"I think you've done enough damage for the moment, just go home, I've got her," James replies, his voice full of hostility.

Okay, spoke too soon clearly. Lying back I put my head on the floor and am about to just let them continue when I hear the familiar clinking of stiletto heels on the floor getting closer, and craning my neck I see a shiny pink heel emerge from around the corner. Oh God, they're perfection. Round toes, shocking pink, satin I think, little straps around the ankles, at least five inches. I suddenly realise that not only has the pain temporarily gone from my leg but I am dragging myself across the floor to get closer to the shoes. I just have to find out where she got them from.

"Sophie, what the bloody hell are you doing?" I look up to see Dan standing over me with an expression of utter bewilderment on his face. Turning back I can't hear them anymore – the most perfect shoes in the world were gone. Bugger!

I allow Dan to lift me back onto the ridiculously small bed and pull up the bar so there's no chance of me falling out again.

"Listen, Soph…"

"I wonder if she was a visitor or a doctor?" I say aloud.

"What?"

"If she was a doctor I can probably find out who she is and ask her where she got them."

"Sophie, please, I'm trying to tell you…"

"But if she's a visitor I might never find them," I say

225

despondently.

"Me and Chloe, we… we are over for good now," he stutters.

Maybe they do them in flats too, like a dolly shoe version, then I could get both and wear the flat ones until my leg… What did he just say?

"What?" I say, staring at him slightly open-mouthed in disbelief.

"Me and Chloe, I told her how I felt about you and well…"

"I, I don't know what to say. Where's James?" I say, suddenly realising that he was no longer in my cubicle.

"He's gone," Dan says distractedly, before repeating himself more animatedly. "He's gone, see? Fucked off and left you again, you can't trust him, Soph, he's no good."

"Say's you." The audacity of the man astounds me. How can he say that? Although he is kind of right, James has disappeared.

"Fifth Avenue," a voice interrupts from the end of the bed, and tearing my eyes away from Dan I see James standing there with a woman standing next to him. Peering closer, I can see she is the woman, the woman with my shoes! He had found her and found my shoes!

"What the…" Dan exclaims, more bewildered than ever.

"When can I get them?" I ask, ignoring Dan completely and never taking my eyes off James.

The woman smiles at me before giving James a squeeze on the arm and walking away, stopping briefly and turning back to say, "You've got yourself a keeper there, darling, a man who understands shoes, that's every woman's dream!" Chuckling to herself she walks away again, and I look back at James, having

226

completely forgotten Dan was in the room.

He takes a step forward and perches on the edge of my bed, holding my hand in his as he leans forwards and almost whispers, "You'll have them in a week," before kissing me lightly on the forehead and sitting up again, never letting go of my hand. I think I have died and gone to heaven – a man who understands the importance of shoes!

Chapter Twenty Four
To choose or not to choose

I don't know whether it was the drugs they gave me or the concussion, or the complete depression at the realisation that I won't be able to wear heels for at least eight weeks, but for some reason I seem to have done the first vaguely sensible thing in my life. Two months ago I broke my leg, had two men fighting over me and a week later had just got hold of the most perfect shoes in existence, and so I told both Dan and James that I needed space and didn't want to see them for a while. I know, for a girl who has spent practically her whole life looking for a man it's pretty drastic to tell them to bugger off when they finally get here, but I think I've done the right thing, I really do, I think!

Anyway, since I told them that, James went back to LA, which wasn't exactly what I was expecting to be honest. I mean, I was kind of hoping that he would refuse to leave, and I did have to get Emily to lock me in the flat and take away my crutches so I couldn't hobble to the airport to find him. Dan stayed but luckily I haven't had to see him either as I've been off work, and he hasn't exactly been knocking my door down, although I have had a few more voicemails than I'm used to, and I may have had my phone confiscated when I was caught hiding it in my cast when Emily walked in, when I was trying to text him.

But today that all changes because my cast is off, although that is a memory I am trying to push to the back of my mind. Seriously, it was disgusting. They took it off and I looked like the hairiest person in the world – my whole leg was just... well... it was horrific, and to top it off my doctor was really kind of cute, too. And there I was laying in front of him trying to flirt, thinking that he may be my ticket out of the whole triangle situation I have somehow got myself into, until I sit up and nearly pass out as I see the yeti's leg where mine used to be. None of that matters today though as I have my life back, my job back and most importantly the ability to wear shoes back!

Turning over lazily, I stretch out and wiggle my toes – freedom! You never do realise how much you take things like legs for granted until they get taken away from you. I tried to wear my beautiful new shoes when they arrived from America, like James had promised they would, but obviously I could only get one of them on. And do you know how difficult it is to walk on crutches with one leg in a cast and the other in a stiletto! Needless to say it ended badly with a few broken pieces of crockery, a mangled stool and a black eye, I always knew that kitchen stool would have a bad end.

Oh shit, it's half seven already, I really should be on my way to work already. Oh well, they can't be too mad at me for being a tiny bit late on my first day back, can they?

* * *

Sitting on the train half an hour later I glance at myself in the reflection of the window opposite, the familiar butterflies rising in my stomach. I've power-dressed today in a pinstripe pencil skirt suit and pale blue shirt, with a high ponytail. I've even kept my make-up neutral, and I have had to opt for a plain pair of court shoes, seeing as I still have a bit of a cankle going on. It better go down soon because I still can't wear half my shoes that have straps on them, and heels are only just coming back into play with me. I know! I haven't been able to wear a pair of stilettos in two months, it has nearly killed me.

It's okay, just breathe, Sophie, just breathe. I mean, so what if I have to see Dan today for the first time in eight weeks? I get to find out where I am going for the next article and that is so much more exciting and much more interesting than a stupid man who messed me around and made me break my leg.

* * *

Walking slowly into the office I feel strange, almost like I've been away for much longer, which is a bit weird really seeing as I barely ever spend more than one day a week in the place, if that! I head towards my desk, stopping to greet people as they ask how I am and, for once, try and deflect the attention away from myself and the embarrassment of the whole situation, as the

230

whole office is bound to know all the gossip and all the sordid little details. Dumping my bag down I spin round on my chair and switch my computer on, before I notice the huge bouquet of roses on my desk. My heart gives a little leap as I remember James's Valentine's gift and then quickly sinks as the memories of Dan's lies also speed to the forefront of my mind. Searching through the flowers, I pick up the little card:

I'm so sorry; I hope I can make it up to you. Dan xx

Okay, well I wasn't expecting that. Leaning back in my chair I take a deep breath and try to work out exactly what the bloody hell is going on here. After two hours of trying in vain to work out what exactly I am supposed to do now, and how I am going to deal with Dan the next time I see him, Marie calls me into her office.

"How's the leg, Sophie?" she says, not even looking up as I sit down in front of her desk.

"Erm, well it's…"

"That's great," she interrupts. Bloody cheek! I don't know why she even bothers to act like she's concerned, everyone knows she hasn't got a heart. "Anyway, this weekend you and Dan are going to St Petersburg, so you need to rest your leg up for the trip. You can work from home for the rest of the week, researching."

"Oh, err okay," I reply, simply getting up and wandering out of the office, even more confused than when I had gone in.

* * *

Four hours later – and I can't say that I'm not glad the day is over – and I am home, complete with roses, card, plane ticket and a very sore head. Walking into the living room Emily confronts me, thrusting a large glass of wine into my hand and guiding me to the sofa. This day is getting weirder by the second.

"What's wrong?" I say bemused.

"Who are the flowers from?"

"Oh these? They're from Dan," I say, leaning forward and setting them on the table, along with the card and plane ticket, when I suddenly notice another envelope sitting on the other side of the table. "What's that?" I ask, looking up at Emily, suddenly suspicious of the wine in my hand.

"I don't know but it's for you… and it's from America," she says, glancing back down at it before picking it up and practically throwing it at me.

"What?" I say astounded, taking a huge gulp of wine. This day is starting to sound like some sort of TV show. Maybe all that wishing to be a soap star has come true and now I'm starring in my very own soap or something. With shaking hands I rip open the envelope, and pull out a handful of loose rose petals, another envelope and a card. Emily gasps and almost bursts into tears – bloody emotional women.

"That's so romantic," she gushes. "What does the card say?"

I take another huge gulp of wine and nearly choke as I pick it up and read it:

"Even though I can't be with you tonight, know that my heart is always by your side."

Wow, that's just about the most romantic thing anyone has ever said to me.

"Oh my God, that's amazing, he's amazing," says Emily, drinking the last of her wine and promptly refilling both glasses.

"So what's in the other envelope?"

"It's a plane ticket to LA!" I gasp incredulously, holding it in my quivering hands.

"And what's the card and stuff from Dan?" she presses, glancing over at the other side of the table, before looking back at me, eyes wide with curiosity.

"It's a card saying sorry and a plane ticket to Russia on... wait a minute... it's on the same bloody day as James's ticket to LA!" I say, sitting back and downing my wine in one.

"So it's simple then, it's time to choose."

"What?"

"It's finally come down to it, you have to pick one, now!" She looks at me, sloshing her wine around in her glass before drinking half of it and refilling both the glasses again.

"How am I supposed to pick?" I say helplessly.

"I know, we weigh up the pros and cons and go from there."

Well okay, that sounds simple enough.

"Okay then, Dan..." I start.

"Right, well pros, he's here for a start, there's no distance involved."

"What's that got to do with anything?"

"Oh come on, James was always a bit of a holiday romance, wasn't he?"

"No, I wasn't even on holiday." Honestly, you'd think she would know that seeing as I live with her.

"Yeah, but he was," she laughs.

"No, he wasn't, he was working," I retaliate.

"Well whatever, he still lives halfway across the bloody planet, doesn't he?"

"Yeah, but his parents live here and he works here all the time, so he spends half the time over here anyway," I argue back, finishing my third glass of wine in as many minutes. I think tonight may get a bit messy.

*　*　*

After two hours of weighing up all the pros and cons of both men we are no closer to picking one; however, we are a lot drunker, and now seem to be quoting random things at each other, which was probably sparked by 'Moulin Rouge', which is now playing rather loudly on the TV, and weighing up the tiniest thing in a vein hope to get closer to a choice.

"Okay, okay," Emily says dramatically, after another giggling fit over nothing. "Which one of them is the best kisser?"

"Oh kissing, hmmm you can tell a lot from a kiss, you know," I say, trying to sound intelligent but only succeeding in slurring my words.

"Like what?" she says, at the same time as opening the third bottle of wine and spilling a load of it all over the table.

"Soul meets soul on lover's lips," I quote, smiling to myself at my ability to say that without getting it all muddled up. Or did I just copy that from the film? No I don't think so, oh I don't know.

"Alright, no need to go all lit… lit… literary on me," she stutters, giggling at her own tipsiness.

"Next question," I shout. "Let me see, I know, which one has apologised for being a dick the most?"

"Ah, but you know what they say," Emily pipes up excitedly.

"What do they say?"

"Love means never having to say you're sorry."

We both fall about laughing and slosh wine all over the carpet. Oops, we may have to buy a new rug, I think.

"So what about James then?" she says, as she regains her composure. "I mean, he left the country, and you barely know him anyway. I mean you've only spent a few weeks with him and you see Dan all the time, so oh, I don't know, I just think that you're taking this whole thing with James too seriously. I'm not saying Dan is the best choice, but well, I guess… just be careful, sweetheart," she says before muttering under her breath, "If he wasn't such an arsehole."

"But absence makes the heart grow fonder," I say, realising too late that that quote didn't really make any sense there, or answer the question, but it made me feel better so who cares.

"Right, so we've got an amazingly romantic, gorgeous, Hollywood dream man, who lives halfway across the world but who does whatever you want and is clearly willing to do anything you ask on the one hand…" She gasps for breath before continuing, "… and on the other hand, we have a man who lives near, and is also pretty hot, but who messed you around, broke your leg, has expected you to give up everything for him, but hasn't been willing to do anything for you."

I have to say that was a pretty compelling argument; the only problem is I think I still love Dan, but I love James too.

"Oh God, I don't know who to pick," I cry in desperation. "I can't do this now, I'll just pick later, I'll pick in the morning," I say, totally exhausted. Saying goodnight to Emily I sway to my room and collapse on my bed, the day's events swirling around in my mind, making the room spin faster.

* * *

Waking up I feel like my head is on fire, and after attempting to get up and get some coffee, I decide the best plan is to go back to sleep.

Three hours later and the pain is little better, but after a cold shower, some painkillers and drinking copious amounts of water and coffee, I still can't quite face doing any research. I mean, if I start researching then that means I have chosen Dan, and I don't think I have, how could I everything is telling me to pick James, he's kind, gentle, loving... good at running away to America, but most importantly he found my shoes without me even having to ask. But there's something in my heart that is still telling me to go to Dan, the man who cheated, lied and betrayed me and also forced me to ruin a beautiful pair of shoes.

Now my head is hurting all over again, Marie did tell me to rest so I think I may just spend the day in front of my 'Gavin and Stacey' DVD, that'll cheer me up.

* * *

Okay, so it's been three days and I feel like a hobo, I think Emily may be staying at Sam's just to avoid me now and even the other girls have stopped calling round. I haven't really moved from the sofa, I haven't even been to get my hair done, which is very unlike me before a big trip, especially my first one in a few months. I can't make a decision and it's killing me, what the bloody hell do I do, my fairy godmother from Ruth's wedding has royally buggered off and left me in the lurch, I even said she could borrow the 'perfect' shoes. My nails are a state and I haven't even started to consider wardrobe options, I'm a complete mess and I go away tomorrow. I really just want one of them to turn up on my doorstep now and make the decision for me, I hate this so much I am absolutely rubbish at making decisions, and they both know that. Hang on a minute I bet this is a set up, some sort of punishment for something, not sure what though, but I bet there in it together, the bastards, I knew it. Well they won't get away with it, maybe I won't pick either of them and cash in the tickets so I can fly to Australia and find myself a gorgeous surfer or something.

Right, time to start packing I think. I pull out my biggest suitcase – the beautiful red one I was forced into buying at Harrods that time – and open it on my bed, standing with my hands on my hips. This could get difficult now – I could be going to Russia, which means jumpers, trousers and boots, but then again I may choose James and head off to the land of little dresses, bikinis and sandals, or better still I'll ditch both and head of anywhere I decide, so which do I pack for?

Maybe I'll attempt it again after some breakfast. So, heading out to the kitchen I make myself some toast and settle down in front of the telly, staring at the screen to avoid looking at the roses and cards on the table.

* * *

Bugger, I leave in about nine hours and not only have I not

decided which direction my life is now going to go in, I still haven't packed! This is not good. Right okay, I have no choice but to just sort this out now, or maybe I could just pack for both occasions. Oh I don't know, this is so confusing and I really hate being confused as it makes me frown, which makes me spend more on anti-wrinkle creams, which makes me frown more – it's a vicious circle. Flicking through my playlists and reaching my 'packing' one, I press play and dance around my room, pulling out clothes left, right and centre. I say dance, my leg is still a bit stiff after the whole breaking it thing, so it's more a case of swaying on the spot and then hopping from place to place. Well, I don't want to injure it again, do I? It's imperative I wear my heels tomorrow, otherwise my travelling outfit is completely ruined.

I have two tickets in my handbag, for two different flights, and I still haven't picked a man. The only good thing is that my packing skills mean that I am packed for any country and just about any weather, so I don't have to choose until I get to the airport. Even my outfit for travelling is layered, so I don't have to change too much if I change my mind either way.

* * *

It's Friday and today is D-Day. Sitting in the car with Dan, I can honestly say I've never been so nervous in all my life. I mean, this is a really big deal, what if I make the wrong decision? The other one is hardly going to wait around for me, is he? Come on, Sophie, just bite the bullet and be a grown-up, this is what you've always wanted, men fighting over you. Mind you, I never knew it would get this complicated.

"You okay?" Dan asks, looking over at me as he parks the car.

"Yeah, yeah, I'm fine," I reply distractedly.

"Listen, I'm sorry, you do believe me, don't you?" he says, once we are waiting in line to check in.

"Yeah, I know you are," I say, Emily's words from the other night suddenly ring in my ears. This is just getting more and more difficult. As I take a step forward, my mind still elsewhere, my foot gets caught in the handle of my bag, and I go flying in one direction as my shoe goes flying in the other. Dan grabs hold of me and I suddenly find myself in his arms. This is like something out of a Hollywood movie. Holding onto him, I can feel him pulling me closer to him, his face so close to mine I can feel his breath on me, my heart racing. Is he the one, am I going to choose him?

"Er hmm."

"Huh?" I stutter, looking around dazedly and slightly angrily at the person who had just interrupted my perfect movie moment.

"You dropped your shoe," a young woman says shyly.

"Oh thanks," I say, taking it from her.

"They're beautiful by the way," she says, before turning and walking the few steps back to her family.

"Oh thanks," I call to her, looking down at my shoe, my perfect shoe, the shoe that James got me. I look back at Dan as he grabs my hand in his, before looking back at the shoe again as I slip it back onto my foot. This is it, I have to say something, I have to say something perfect. Come on, Sophie, think! A quote, that's it, a quote, something I was saying with Emily the other night, but what? Think, Sophie, think!

"Soph?" Dan's voice breaks through my thoughts and I look into his eyes, his beautiful, lying eyes.

"You know what, Dan?" I say, having no idea what will come out of my mouth next. "I can't do this."

"What do you mean? Isn't this what you wanted, us going away together?" he replies looking dumbfounded.

I almost laugh at him, but I don't because he looks so beautiful in his tight jeans and shirt.

"If you really loved someone you would be willing to give up everything for them, but if they loved you back they'd never ask you to." Wow, that was quite good really, bloody brilliant actually! Who knew my brain could come up with something like that? Oh crap, yeah, I have to follow it through with something instead of just standing in front of him. Picking up the handle of my case and pulling the ticket out of my pocket, I take one last look into his gorgeous face before walking away, smiling to myself.

One Year Later...

"I've never really been the kind of girl to settle down and play second to anyone; I always thought I'd be the famous one and have my man following me around. But when you find somebody who can read your mind even in the middle of an argument at a hospital bed, and then go and find you the most perfect pair of shoes in the world and fly them halfway across the planet for you, well you have to make allowances, don't you?" I breathe slowly and look up at the woman sitting in front of me and receive a nod.

"That was perfect, Mrs Hanson," she says, closing her notebook, and I smile, glancing over at James.

God, this reminds me of that bloody awful dating agency video I recorded – it seems like forever ago that I did that. A warm glow fills me from my head right to the tips of my beautiful new Jimmy Choos as he grins back at me, and I think about how different this video has turned out. I wonder if anyone ever responded to my dating thingy? Mind you, I don't really care. I've found the perfect man: a man who not only understands me but a man who understands... shoes!

About the Author

Natalie-Jane Revell was born twenty three years ago in Harlow, Essex, where she was brought up, before moving to Bath to complete a degree in Creative Writing in English. She has since moved back to her home town, where she spends her days working and saving for her next trip somewhere inspirational.

From a young age Natalie-Jane had a fascination with writing and started writing everything she observed around her, this has led to a love of observational humour which she tries to portray through her writing.

She has also been lucky enough to travel all over the world, gathering inspiration, along with new shoes, from every country, city and town she has visited. An obsession with shopping and shoes soon developed which combined with her want to travel anywhere and everywhere led her to the only possible conclusion; the 'Foot Loose' series.

Around the World in Flip-Flops

Bailey Madison has followed her dreams all the way to… Cornwall!

The beach is not exactly the tropical paradise that she originally envisaged, but are things about to change dramatically in Baileys life, as a chance encounter sends her on an epic journey around the globe in search of her happily ever after scenario.

Her best friend is already being swept into her own whirlwind romantic journey leaving Bailey in the world alone with no one to show her the way.

Just when things couldn't get any worse she is sidetracked by not one, but three men confusing her emotions and complicating her mind.

Bailey thought she had it all figured out; find '*that*' man, live by '*that*' sea and live out '*that*' life… it was planned and perfect. Just one problem, the man she thinks is 'The One' takes her away from '*that*' dream, leaving her with the endless dilemma, is he the right one after all?

But most importantly how will the girl that only knows sand in her hair, bikinis and her trusty flip flops cope away from the the place she loves… the beach?

Due 2011